COAST TO COAST

WYNCOTE WOLVES
BOOK SEVEN

CALI MELLE

To all the girlies who just want to be told they are a good girl.

PROLOGUE
STELLA

Sitting on the couch, I glance over at Simon whose eyes are glued to mine. A smirk tugs on the corner of his mouth and he remains silent as he raises a finger to his lips. My brother, Sterling, is arguing with his girlfriend, Olivia, about the movie we just watched. I let out a yawn, lifting my arms up as I stretch out my spine.

My eyes glance back and forth between the two of them as they both rise to their feet. I'm not even paying attention to their futile argument anymore. It's still kind of weird, seeing my brother and my best friend in a relationship, but honestly, I don't think that there is anyone better for either of them.

"Look," I start as I grab one of the blankets draped over the back of the couch and pull it down onto my lap. "I'm pretty damn tired and you guys are in my bedroom right now. Care to take this somewhere else?"

Simon coughs to cover up his laugh as Sterling and Olivia both turn to look at me. Sterling narrows his eyes, giving me his infamous dirty look, while Olivia smiles at me.

"I'm so sorry, Stell," she says, her voice soft and gentle as she slides her hand into Sterling's. "We'll go upstairs so you can get some sleep. And maybe then your brother will come to his senses and agree with me."

"Doubtful," Sterling grumbles, shaking his head as he follows after Olivia. "The ending was done artfully. It leaves it open to each viewer's interpretation."

"No way," Olivia scoffs, rolling her eyes at him. "There needed to be more closure."

The two of them disappear upstairs and a sigh slips from my lips as I unfold the blanket and lay it across my body. Grabbing one of the pillows that they gave me to use, I tuck it in the corner of the sectional couch and flop down, pulling the blanket with me. Lifting my head, I glance over at Simon, who is sitting there with an eyebrow cocked.

"You want me to leave?" he questions me, his voice hoarse as his steel gray eyes search mine.

I swallow roughly and shake my head. "You can stay, as long as you're quiet."

"And what if I'm not?"

"Then you can go to your room too," I tell him. "Believe it or not, it's exhausting sleeping on a couch every night."

Simon stares at me for a moment and I'm lost in the metallic color of his eyes. "You can take my bed and I'll sleep down here."

A soft laugh escapes me and I shake my head at him. "I appreciate the offer, but I only have a few more days here, so it's not that big of a deal. I'm ready to head back to California, though."

Simon's eyebrows pull together slightly. "You grew up on the East Coast, right? What's so special about the west?"

"Nothing special," I reply with a shrug, attempting to get more comfortable on the couch. "It's just a lot different there. Nothing seems to slow down whereas it almost feels like we move on island time here. And it's much warmer."

"Yuck." Simon's face contorts. "How are you supposed to play lake hockey then?"

Rolling my eyes, I shake my head at him as

another laugh escapes me. "Such a one-track mind... You skate indoors, like normal people."

"That's boring."

I raise an eyebrow at him, a smirk playing on my lips. "You're boring."

Simon's tongue darts out as he wets his lips and my gaze is instantly drawn to the act. "I'm far from boring, baby. You want me to show you?"

"Nice try, Simon, but I'm not falling for that one."

He simply shrugs as he rises to his feet. My eyes widen as he begins to move over to me. He stops beside the couch, hovering above me. Rolling onto my back, our gazes collide and my breath catches in my throat. The way his dark hair hangs in waves down to his ears is distracting me.

He's been my brother's roommate for almost two years. I'm not blind, so of course I've noticed him every damn time I've been here. That doesn't change anything. The furthest we've ever gone was flirting, and I can't let it go past that. As fun as it would be, I have an entire life in California... which includes a boyfriend.

"What are you doing, Simon?" I whisper as he bends down, caging me in with his hands on either side of my head.

He tilts his head to the side, his steel eyes burning holes through mine. There's a look of mischief in his gaze that melts with something indistinguishable. Suddenly, he pulls the pillow out from under my head. My head lifts up before falling back onto the couch in a rush.

Simon stands back up, clutching the pillow as a soft chuckle vibrates in his chest. My face contorts, my eyes slicing to his.

"What the hell was that for?"

He tosses the pillow onto the other side of the sectional as a smirk pulls on his lips. "That's my pillow and you're in my spot."

My eyebrows tug together as I abruptly sit up. "What are you talking about? I've been sleeping here the past week, using that pillow that my brother gave me to use."

Simon shakes his head at me. "You're sleeping in my bed until you leave. I'll take the couch."

"No thanks," I shake my head, attempting to stay strong against his persistence. "I'm not sleeping between your dirty-ass sheets that you've had other girls in."

Simon raises an eyebrow at me. "Are you jealous, Stella?"

"Absolutely not," I lie through my teeth, cringing. "I have a boyfriend, just so you know."

Simon snorts. "Like that really means anything."

I stare back at him in disbelief. The audacity of this asshole. I don't know if I should be more offended that he thinks I would cheat on my boyfriend or if I should be pissed off at his cockiness. Like he can get any girl he wants. Ignoring Simon, I rise to my feet, abandoning my spot on the couch as I walk around the back of it.

"Where are you going?"

I glance at him as I pause in the doorway. "To get some sleep since you won't leave me alone."

The corners of Simon's lips lift. "Ah, so you can follow directions."

I scoff, rolling my eyes before turning my back to him as I begin to exit the room.

"Stella," I hear his voice call out from where he's now laying on the couch. Turning around, I look back at him again with slight irritation written across my expression. "For the record, my sheets are clean. No other girl has ever been in my bed."

My breath catches in my throat as his steel gray eyes burn holes through mine from across the room. My heart pounds erratically in my chest, my lips parting, but words fail me. Instead, I simply nod before spinning on my heel and hightailing it out of the living room.

God forbid I stick around here any longer.

I might do something stupid... like ask him to join me in his bed.

CHAPTER ONE
STELLA

It feels strange, flying back to California after I had just spent the past week at my brother's house. He's a total grump, but I missed being around him. And now that he's dating my best friend, it's like a win-win. He finally has someone who makes him happy and I get to see both of them a hell of a lot more.

Well, only when I'm in Vermont.

Instead, I'm flying back to the West Coast, where I've been building a new life for the past year. I have a few weeks left of my freshman year and then I'll be flying back to Vermont to spend the summer there. It was my brother's idea and when he offered his apartment, I wasn't about to say no.

Sterling and Olivia are finally moving out and

they are getting their own place. That will leave an empty room where he's living with two of his team-mates, Simon Murray and Lincoln Reid. Vermont isn't my favorite place to be, but I don't have anywhere to stay on the West Coast for the summer. My best friend here, Helena, and I had talked about getting a place but never went through with it.

My flight was a few hours earlier than antici-pated after they had some last-minute changes. I decided that I would just come home early so I could stop by Trey's place on my way home. I didn't bother telling Trey about it and I didn't tell him when I got to California since it was supposed to be a surprise for him.

He had given me a key to his place a few weeks before I left for Vermont. I tried to get him to come along with me but he said he wasn't able to take the time off from work. I didn't push the issue. We were still new. Three months of being in a relationship isn't very long, especially when you're trying to navigate the early years of college.

It still bothered me a little bit. I wanted him to be with me. He made sure to call me every day and text me while I was gone, so that made it a little better. After I got through the first few days in Vermont, it didn't bother me as much. Simon had an uncanny way of distracting me, although I shouldn't think of him that way.

Especially not when I'm standing out in front of my boyfriend's apartment door.

Sliding my key into the lock, I turn it to the side and let myself into his place. It's quiet and with how early it is in the morning, I'm sure Trey is still in bed. He works for a tech company, but he gets to make his own hours since he's salary. He's the type of person who works better at night and is the furthest thing from a morning person.

Quietly closing the door behind me, I leave my suitcase by the front door and kick off my shoes before I make my way through his apartment. As I walk past the dining room area, I notice there are still dishes on the table from what must have been his dinner from last night. But instead of there only being one plate, there are two. Two plates. Two wineglasses.

My stomach sinks and I inch closer to the table, grabbing one of the glasses. As I lift it into the air in front of my face, I notice the lipstick stains around the rim of the glass. The air leaves my lungs in a rush and I feel the bile beginning to rise up my throat.

Part of me wants to give him the benefit of the

doubt. Maybe he just had a friend over last night and forgot to clean up before he went to bed. The other part of me knows Trey doesn't have any female friends. And definitely not any he would have over for dinner without me here.

Fuck.

Just like that, the pieces start to fall into place and suddenly, everything makes sense. Trey didn't want to come with me because I wasn't the only one. He wanted to stay home so he could sneak around with whoever he was seeing behind my back.

His bedroom door opens and I slowly turn around, holding my breath as my grip tightens around the stem of the wineglass. I'm ready to face Trey, but then the rug is ripped out from underneath my feet as Helena—my best fucking friend—walks out of my boyfriend's bedroom wearing nothing but one of his t-shirts.

She stops in her tracks in the center of the hallway as she sees me. The wineglass falls from my hands, shattering as it crashes into the wood floor. Helena's eyes widen and a flash of panic and guilt washes over her.

"Oh my god!" she exclaims loudly as she begins to take a step toward me.

"What's wrong, baby?" Trey says to her as he walks out into the hallway, running his hand through his dirty blond hair. His gaze follows Helena's and lands on me.

It's like all the air is instantly drained from the room. I can't fucking move, but I know I need to. My stomach rolls and I want to vomit all over his hardwood fucking floors.

"It's not what it looks like, Stella," Trey says quickly as he moves away from my best friend and begins to walk in my direction. "Helena came over and one thing led to another."

I back away, shaking my head at him. "Don't even bother, Trey. Save your bullshit for someone else who will believe it." I turn my attention to Helena, who looks both horrified and equally hurt. "I can't believe you would do this to me."

"Stell," she says softly as she steps up beside Trey. "It wasn't supposed to happen like this and I didn't know how the hell to tell you."

I stare at her in disbelief, a choked laugh escaping me. "Well, for starters, you could have avoided fucking my boyfriend."

"Stella." Trey's voice is strained, like he's torn between what to do. Who he should choose. "Let's just talk about this, okay?

"There's nothing to talk about," I tell him as I make my way over to my suitcase. Part of me is in complete and utter shock. The other part of me just wants to disappear and never see either of them for the rest of my life. I can't believe this happened. "I just want to know... how long has this been going on?"

Helena glances over at Trey, like she doesn't want to be the one who tells me the truth. Trey's lips purse and he hangs his head in defeat. "About two months."

My breath catches in my throat. "We've only been together for three. You've been sleeping with my best friend behind my back, like, the entire time we've been together?"

"We slept together before the two of you started dating," Helena adds in, almost as if she's defending herself and validating them doing this. I can see it in Helena's expression that this is killing her and it isn't because of what they did to me. It's because of what she's afraid to lose.

She wants him to herself and me knowing what was happening between them threatens that.

"You can have him, Helena," I tell her as I slide Trey's key from my keyring. Tossing it onto the counter, I look at my now ex-boyfriend once more. "Fuck you for this. Fuck you both, actually."

"Stella, wait," Trey interjects, but I shake my head at him and watch Helena reach out for him with her manicured hand wrapping around his wrist.

"Let her go, babe," she says simply, and I can taste the fucking vomit on the back of my tongue.

"Yeah, babe," I sneer at him. "Let me go. This is over. I never want to hear from either of you again. You both deserve each other."

There's so much more I want to say to the two of them but I can feel the emotion welling inside. I've been holding my composure because in reality, Trey doesn't mean that much. What he did doesn't hurt me nearly as much as what Helena did and how she's acting.

It just proves she was never my friend to start with.

I slip outside of his apartment, taking my suit-case with me. The betrayal hits me like a ton of bricks and the tears blur my vision as I head back out to the front of the apartment building to order an Uber. Part of me wants to take it back to the airport instead of my dorm.

For the first time in my life, I actually feel home-sick. I never thought I would see the day, because I was not built for the cold. And even though I had lived in Vermont my entire life, I never did adjust to it. It's not the place that I miss, though... it's the people.

My brother is a complete pain in my ass, but I miss being around him. I miss his grumpy attitude and giving him shit. My best friend, Olivia. I swear, that girl couldn't be more polar opposite than me, but she's practically my soulmate. I hated when we first separated after high school to go our separate ways for college, but every time I see her, it sucks leaving her even more.

And then there's Simon.

I shouldn't even be thinking of him, but I almost feel like a weight has been lifted since Trey is gone from my life now. Losing Helena hurts more than the failed relationship. It's not like we were together that long. I may have had an attachment, but it's nothing I won't be able to move on from.

Thoughts of Simon are a welcomed distraction, even if my brother's roommate loves to grate on my nerves. Things are easy with him, almost as if we are old friends. He and my brother have lived together for a couple years now, so he's become a constant when I go back to Vermont. I never thought I would see the day where I was feeling like I was missing him, but here we are.

I didn't get to talk to him this morning because I left in the early hours of the day, well before he was awake. And there was a weird part of me that didn't want to say goodbye to him. He's a total flirt and I honestly love it. Sure, he's annoying. But there's something about him I thoroughly enjoy. Perhaps it is the banter and how he keeps me on my toes.

Or maybe it's the way he looks at me with those metallic eyes of his.

He might be one of my favorite people to be around when I'm back in my hometown.

And I'll be spending all summer with him.

CHAPTER TWO
SIMON

I'm sitting alone in the living room when I hear Sterling and Lincoln upstairs moving around. Lincoln had just moved in with us this past year after Vaughn moved out. After his accident, things really went south for him. He moved back in with his parents because of the intense recovery he was going to have. He had been dodging everyone's calls and refused to see any of us. It was almost as if his hockey career was over so he said fuck you to the rest of us.

We all knew it wasn't like that, though. He just went through a life changing event. I couldn't even imagine how I would react or respond after something like that. One moment, you're moving up in the hockey world and the next, it's completely gone.

We had to give him some grace and thankfully his mother kept us all in the loop with his recovery.

He was doing well but still had a long road ahead of him.

After he moved out, we had an open room and Lincoln just so happened to be looking for somewhere to move. It kind of worked out, even if there was a somberness to Vaughn missing from the picture.

I completely get it. I just don't know that I would be one of those guys.

A lot of the guys on our team are graduating this year, including Sterling. That means he'll be moving out, but not just because he and Olivia are getting their own place. He'll be moving on to the next chapter in his life, along with August, Logan, Hayden, and Asher. We were losing a lot of guys, but we've been working with our newer players to try and get them ready to go.

Lincoln is just a freshman, so I'll have one more year here with him and then I'll be off to hopefully follow the rest of my friends. I would imagine that we'll have someone else move in with us after Sterling is gone, but that's not something I really want to think about right now. He's one of my closest friends and not just because we've been living together since I was in my sophomore year. He was the one who took me under his wing when I was a freshman—just like I've been doing with Lincoln.

It's this strange little brotherhood, but it's almost better than a blood-related family. And I'm not just saying that because mine sucks.

Sterling is the first to make his way downstairs. I've been sitting down here for the past hour. I woke up earlier than normal and just couldn't fall back asleep. So, I came down here to do the same thing I was doing in my room. Sitting, staring at the wall while contemplating life.

"Oh shit," Sterling jumps when he walks into the living room and finds me on the couch. "What are you doing awake already?"

I glance over at him and shrug. "Couldn't sleep."

"Is everything okay?" he questions me, his eyebrows drawn together. It isn't often Sterling really gives a shit about anyone. It's not that he doesn't care—he's just one of those people who walks around with blinders on. He only sees and pays attention to what he wants. And one of the only things he actually cares about is Olivia.

"Yeah, just got some weird shit floating around in my head," I tell him with a look of indifference. "I usually get a little weird during this in-between period—when the season ends and waiting for summer league to start. Not to mention, it's weird thinking about all of you guys graduating soon."

Sterling tilts his head to the side. "You saying you're going to miss me, Murray?"

I nod, unashamed of our little bromance. "Damn straight. We've lived together the past two years. What the hell am I going to do with just Lincoln?"

This earns a laugh from Sterling. "You guys will manage. I'm not leaving your life forever, Simon. Don't get all sappy and shit on me now."

"What are you going to do if I cry at graduation?"

Sterling cocks an eyebrow. "Pretend like I have no idea who the fuck you are."

"What are the two of you going on about?" Lincoln cuts in as he walks into the living room, brushing past Sterling.

"Sterling said if I cry at graduation, he's going to pretend like he doesn't know me."

Lincoln drops down onto the other side of the couch, giving me a weird look. "You guys are really strange. Like I know you have your own little bromance, but sometimes I wonder if it's more than that."

Sterling chokes out a laugh, shaking his head.

"Hell no. Which, speaking of... I think I'm going to propose to Olivia after graduation."

"I'm surprised you haven't put a ring on it already," I tell him, smiling at my friend. "Where is she, anyways? It's weird with her not being here."

"She had finals to study for so she wanted to sleep at her dorm this week. She'll be back then."

"Thank God," Lincoln sighs, propping his hands behind his head. "She's a much better cook than the two of you guys, and my bank account is going to cry if I have to start ordering from DoorDash again every day."

Sterling gives Lincoln the middle finger. "My girlfriend isn't your own personal chef." He slices his eyes at him with his infamous grumpy attitude before disappearing into the kitchen. That's just the way Sterling is, even if he doesn't mean any harm or ill intention. Thankfully, it didn't take Lincoln long to realize this.

Lincoln glances over at me, shrugging. "If she's here and she's going to cook, then I'm going to eat it."

A laugh rumbles in my chest and I shake my head at him. He's a nice addition to our household dynamic, even if he does irritate Sterling. To be honest, I find it hilarious and it's a nice distraction from the shit swirling around in my head. At least I won't be here completely alone after most of my friends leave me behind.

"Heard that, asshole," Sterling replies gruffly from wherever he is in the kitchen. "Oh and, Simon, can you do me a favor?"

"Sure, what's up?"

Sterling pops his head through the doorway. "Stella is flying back in at the end of next week. She's coming in for graduation and decided she wants to spend the summer back here instead of in California. Something happened with her piece-of-shit boyfriend but she wouldn't tell me."

My ears perk up, my heart instantly hammering in my chest. "Where's she staying?"

"Okay, that was something else I wanted to talk to you guys about..." Sterling's voice trails off as he steps into the room again. "After graduation, I decided I'm going to go to Minnesota to play in this shortened league until the draft. Then, if I get a call, I'll be going wherever the team needs me to be."

"Wait, so you're just, like, *leaving* leaving after graduation?"

Sterling nods. "I mean, kind of. I found somewhere that Olivia and I can lease monthly so if we have to move abruptly, we aren't locked into a year-long thing."

I stare back at my friend. I knew this day was going to be coming, but color me shocked. There shouldn't be any surprise. He's ready to settle down with Olivia and potentially get drafted into the NHL. There's no reason for me to feel as sad as I do at this moment.

"Would it be cool with you guys if Stella stayed here for the summer? She'd be going back to California sometime in August. If not, she can stay at our parents' house instead."

Stella's going to be here for the entire summer.

Living under the same roof as me.

"I'm good with it," I tell him, glancing over at Lincoln who looks like he's about to fall back asleep.

He mumbles something and nods before his eyes close completely and he begins to snore.

"You sure she won't be an issue? She just wanted to come back home for a little bit and I figured she could just take my room while I'm not here."

"Stella's never an issue, dude."

I'm still sad my friend's going to be leaving so soon, but at the same time, knowing his little sister is moving in has me looking forward to something entirely different. I like Stella. There's something about her that piques my interest, even if she gives me goddamn blue balls. I like her personality and sassy attitude. She doesn't take my shit.

She makes things fun, and fun is exactly what I need this summer.

"Are you able to pick her up from the airport next Thursday?"

I smile up at Sterling. "Absolutely."

CHAPTER THREE
STELLA

The last week of my freshman year went by in a flash. I had seen Trey a few times and I wasn't surprised when I saw that he was there to pick up Helena. It hurt like hell and he was a fucking asshole for doing that behind my back. I was done with both of them and was trying to force myself to not give a shit about what was going on between the two of them.

The last thing I wanted to do was have that negativity in my life.

Surprisingly, I experienced a new type of defiance. Usually, I would resort to my normal ways of drinking the pain away, but I wasn't going to let Trey or Helena have that much power over me. He is nothing in my life as far as I am concerned. The last thing he's going to see is the effect of knowing I was cheated on.

I had already spent a majority of my freshman year going to various parties. It has always been the way I was programmed since high school. As soon as I discovered drinking and stuff, I was practically a loose cannon. If there was a party, I was going to be there and I would most likely be ending the night completely trashed.

My brother hated it. My family equally hated it too. And Olivia was always so concerned. She was the one who kept me safe when we were together, so when we split to go to separate colleges, she was really concerned about what was going on with me in California. Olivia constantly worried about anything and everything possible and I was one of the things that occupied that type of space in her mind.

I hated that I put everyone through so much shit with my partying. It's not like I was trying to do it from a malicious place; it wasn't like it was for attention or because I was trying to escape something from my reality. I just felt like parties were somewhere I fit in and I was looking for my own thing like Sterling had hockey. I don't know how to explain it, but after visiting my brother and Olivia, I had a weird change of heart.

One of the nights I was there, Olivia sat me down and expressed her concerns. She didn't get my brother involved but she let me know that he was worried about me too. What they didn't know was, I actually was partying less when I was seeing Trey. He wasn't really into that scene. Even though we would go to some together, he didn't really enjoy drinking, so we spent a lot of weekends skipping the parties.

It just seemed like whenever Olivia or Sterling randomly called me out of the blue, I happened to be out. Since I came back after having that conversation with her, I haven't been to a single party. Hell, I haven't even drank anything. Which, to be honest, I didn't need it after my breakup with Trey, but it would have been nice because I was bored as fuck.

As much as I love California, there was a nostalgia when I was home this last time. And summers in Vermont were always my favorite. It doesn't get quite as hot as it does here in California.

And my mother was begging me to come back since she hadn't gotten to see much of me within this past year. There was a weird strain that was put on our relationship when I graduated high school. I spent the majority of that summer partying and actually got into some trouble, but thankfully she was able to get me out of it.

That's why Sterling was the one I called when I was in trouble or needed something. The last thing I wanted to do was be even more of a burden on my family. That night I got in trouble, I think I broke my mother's heart. She knew I was drinking a lot and I refused to listen to a word she said.

Call it defiance; call it whatever you want. I know I didn't have a bad childhood and I got enough attention from my parents, but I feel like a lot of it had to do with my brother. They invested so much time in Sterling and what he wanted to do. My dreams didn't go ignored, but in a way, I lacked motivation. What could I possibly do that would come remotely close to what he was doing and how happy it made my parents?

Instead, I decided to be the fuckup and enjoy my life. I wasn't going to exert any extra energy doing something that was just going to be outshined by my brother anyway. So, I started partying. And then I got arrested for underage drinking. My mother picked me up at the station that night and was able to get me out of it all with just some community service.

I was forever grateful for her doing that and the fact that she didn't tell my father. It was like it was our own little secret. Even Sterling didn't know. But it put a strain on the relationship I had with my mother. She realized then that she literally had zero control over me, so when I decided I wanted to go to California for school, I couldn't tell if she was happy or sad.

I needed a change of pace. I needed to get away from everything I was used to and try to figure out who I was instead of just Stella Barrett. There was more to me than being the little sister of the star hockey player of our town. I just knew I had to get away from everyoneuber I had been around my entire life to try and figure that out.

And here I am, my freshman year of college finished and I still have no idea who the hell I am.

California helped me realize that I actually really enjoy the ocean. I started school undecided but eventually decided to settle on marine biology. It wasn't a random decision either. After going out on boats and exploring the ocean with Trey and his friends, I realized I found what I really wanted to do.

I don't really have a plan on what I want to do with that, but I want to do something that involves the ocean. Something about the water calls to me on a spiritual level and there's nothing that is going to stop me from following that calling.

As my Uber pulls up out in front of the airport, I thank him and grab my two suitcases before heading inside the building. After getting through security, I send my brother a message telling him I'll be boarding my plane soon and am on my way back to Vermont.

He texts me back just as I'm getting into my seat, telling me how everyone can't wait for me to get here. And then at the end of his message, he throws in one little line that makes my heart skip a beat.

Sterling: Simon will be picking you up when you get here.

After my disaster with Trey, I should be swearing off guys entirely. I have no reason to get involved with anyone, especially when I'm in the process of self-discovery. This summer should be dedicated to figuring out who I am and focusing on nothing else.

When Sterling offered me his apartment, he told me how he wouldn't be around for most of the summer, so that meant I could have his room. It seemed like the perfect plan. I would still be close enough to visit my mother, but could have the space I needed from her. We would be able to repair our relationship without having the strain of breathing down each other's necks.

It also meant that I would now be living with Simon. The idea seemed like a good one when I first agreed to it, but that was before I realized how much he worked his way under my skin. He occupies all of the secret spaces inside my mind and I want him out of there. Just because he lives rent-free inside my mind doesn't mean I have to entertain any of the thoughts that spring upon me.

A sigh slips from my lips as my heart continues to pound erratically inside my chest. I'm excited to see him, but I know I can't let him get any closer. I have to draw the line at flirting and be okay with that. I could have my fun with him and then go back to my normal life, but that defeats the whole purpose of my journey of self-discovery.

Sitting deeper into my seat on the airplane, I let out another deep breath and lean my head against the window as my eyelids fall shut.

This is going to be one hell of a long summer...

CHAPTER FOUR
SIMON

It's late in the afternoon as I pull up to the airport and find a parking spot along the curb. Sterling told me Stella's plane will be landing around four-thirty, so I arrived a few minutes early, just in case. The last thing I wanted was for her to be standing out here waiting by herself. Knowing Stella, she wouldn't subject herself to that. She'd find a ride before waiting for anyone.

Leaving the engine running, I climb out of my car and stand along the side of it on the sidewalk as I wait for her. Part of me wishes I would have brought one of those obnoxious signs, just to embarrass her. I would love to see the redness of her cheeks as I held it up and called out her name.

There's something about Stella that makes me

love to get a reaction out of her. I don't have much of a filter as it is, but it seems like when she's around, I really have no issue with saying whatever the fuck I want to. And she takes it all in stride, throwing it all back in my face in any way she can.

The doors slide open and I see her coming through. She looks like she had a plane ride from hell with the scowl on her face as her suitcase wheel gets stuck in the track of the glass door. A smile touches my lips and I push away from the car, striding over to her.

Stella curses under her breath, abandoning her second suitcase as she fights with the first one. I pause in front of her for a second, watching with amusement as she shoves the thing around, attempting to free it from the track. She's having no such luck, so I decide to step in.

"Let me get that for you."

Her head whips up to look at me, her eyes wide. Realization washes over her expression and I see a pink tint creeping across her cheeks. It isn't the rose color I wanted to see, but seeing her face come to life is enough to make my heart pound. She steps out of the way, throwing her hands up in defeat.

"These damn doors might be the stupidest thing. They know people have suitcases with wheels. Why wouldn't they have something more practical?"

I tilt my head at her as I put my hands on either side of the suitcase and jerk it from side to side. It comes free and I lift it away from the doorway, where a few people are waiting to get through. It feels like she has crammed her entire life in it with how heavy it is.

"Did you have a bad flight?"

Stella's eyes slice to mine before she rolls them, her nostrils flaring as she exhales deeply. "The worst. I just had the biggest dose of birth control ever," she mumbles, shaking her head as she lifts her fingers to her temples. "Five and a half hours on a plane that must have been advertised to just parents. There were seriously so many babies and toddlers on there. Those creatures shouldn't be allowed on planes."

"Was it really that bad?"

She narrows her eyes at me. "There was a couple with an infant next to me. That thing managed to puke everywhere, shit all up its back, and cry on and off within five and a half hours. Yes, it was bad."

A chuckle rumbles in my chest as I take both of her suitcases and lead the way to my car. I haven't really seen this side of Stella. I've heard her and Sterling get into it, but seeing her frustration firsthand is extremely amusing. I shouldn't be smiling at her the way I am right now, but I can't help it.

"What's so funny, Simon?" she questions me, her tone biting. She follows me to the trunk, standing there as she crosses her arms defensively over her chest as I put her things inside.

Grabbing the door, I pull it down to close the trunk before turning to look at her. "Nothing. You're just something else."

"What does that even mean?"

I simply shrug. "Nothing bad. Just chill out and get in the car."

"Fuck that," she argues, now shifting into something more abrasive. There are a lot more layers to Stella Barrett than I realized. And I'm more than willing to peel them all back one at a time. "You're laughing at me and I'm not getting into your car until you tell me why."

"Jesus Christ," I mutter, shaking my head at her. She's absolutely impossible right now. "It was nothing bad. I've never seen you this flustered before so it was amusing."

"Oh, so now I'm amusing?"

I stare at her silently, a little taken back by the way she's reacting. "Dude, chill out."

"I am not your dude."

"Clearly," I mumble, walking around the car before stopping by the passenger's side. I pull the door open and look back at her. "I told you why I was laughing. Are you done with your little temper tantrum so we can go now?"

Stella doesn't move at first and her feet are cemented in place as she attempts to stand her ground. That flight must have really been fucking terrible to have her in a mood like this. I like her fiery attitude, but damn... the heat that is radiating from her feels like it might melt my skin.

She huffs and uncrosses her arms before walking over to the car. I watch her, raising an eyebrow as she drops down into the seat and pulls the door shut behind her. As I walk around the front of the car, I can only hope that something shifts Stella's mood because this is going to be a long-ass summer if she's going to be like this.

Then again... I could always make it fun. Maybe distract her from what's really bothering her.

That is, if she decides to let me.

———

Stella falls asleep on the car ride back to the house. It's about a thirty-minute drive, so as soon as she's knocked out, I let her go. There's no sense in waking her up and honestly, I'm a little afraid to. It seems like it would be a wise decision not to. It would be like waking up a bear right now.

And Stella is a bear, and I don't want to be on the receiving end of her frustration right now.

As I pull the car into the driveway, I put it in park and kill the engine before turning to look at her. She looks so peaceful, her face completely relaxed as she snores lightly. I can't help but be captivated as my eyes explore her features. Her straight nose is turned up slightly at the end. Her cheekbones are high and pronounced.

Everything about her is goddamn perfect—she looks like a sculpture I want inside my house to admire every single day.

Quietly opening my door, I slip out of the car and make my way back to the trunk to get her stuff. I might as well let her sleep a little while longer and take her things inside rather than disturb her right now. I close the trunk, careful to not make any noise after pulling her suitcases out. The car rocks slightly as I push the door down and when I walk past, I glance inside at Stella.

She's still passed out, so I let her be and take her things into the house. Lincoln is sitting on the couch, watching baseball, and Olivia and Sterling are in the kitchen. They both walk out to greet me, confusion passing through their expressions when they see me with Stella's suitcases but no Stella.

"Where's my sister?" Sterling questions me, his eyebrows drawn together.

I motion out to the car. "She's passed out in there and I would advise to approach her with caution. She was in a foul-ass mood when I picked her up at the airport."

"Did she say what was wrong?" Olivia asks me as Sterling sighs.

"She was complaining about the flight. With the way she fell asleep immediately in the car, I think it's safe to say she was cranky and needed to take a nap."

Lincoln laughs from the couch and Sterling shakes his head.

"My bad, dude," he says, his voice full of regret. "Stella can be a little... difficult sometimes. Especially when there's something that's bothering her. She has a little trouble reeling it in."

"Some things will never change, huh?" Olivia muses out loud, smiling at Sterling before winking at him. She isn't wrong. Sterling and Stella are definitely siblings and share more qualities than they'd like to admit. At least Stella isn't a constant grump like Sterling.

She's very close to him, though, with the way she just acted.

"I'll go wake her up," Olivia offers as she brushes past Sterling and me. "If there's anyone she's not going to be pissed off at, it will be me."

I look at Sterling who simply shrugs as Olivia disappears out the front door. "Do you want me to take her bags up to your room?"

Sterling nods. "Yeah. Olivia and I are going to go stay at our new place tonight since we have everything moved in there now. I would hate to see Stella try to get those up the stairs by herself."

A chuckle slips from my lips. "You should have seen her at the airport when the wheel of one of them got stuck in the track of the door."

"Oh Jesus," Sterling groans, shaking his head. "I can only imagine how that did not go well."

"Not at all," I laugh.

"Your sister sounds like quite the spitfire when she's pissed off," Lincoln says to Sterling from where he's sitting on the couch.

"Yeah, I would advise to stay the fuck away from

her," Sterling snaps at him. "If I find out that you've come anywhere near my sister, I'll chop your dick off."

Lincoln throws his hands up in the air in defense. "Got it. She's off-limits."

"Why do I feel like I'm going to regret letting her live here with the two of you?" Sterling says out loud but he directs his attention back to me. There's something in his expression I can't put my finger on, but I don't question it. Especially since he only seemed concerned with Lincoln being interested in her.

I shrug. "Stella is a big girl. She can make her own decisions."

"Yeah, she can, can't she..." Sterling's voice trails off as he cocks an eyebrow at me. "I know she was in your bed the last time she stayed here."

My eyes widen and I stare at him in partial shock. How the fuck could he possibly know that she was in there? And now he has the wrong idea, because she wasn't in there for that reason. I let her sleep in there so she didn't have to sleep on the couch anymore.

As my lips part, I can feel her behind me.

"So what if I was in his bed? Are you going to try and control me like the rest of our family?"

Sterling stares at her over my shoulder, his eyes narrowed slightly. "Nope. You can fuck your life up all by yourself."

There's tension that hangs heavily in the air and an awkward shift. I don't know what is going on between the two of them, but this isn't the reunion I was expecting. With the silence that falls around all of us, I don't think this was what anyone was expecting.

"Thanks, big bro," Stella muses from behind me. "That's very kind of you. And for the record, I was in Simon's bed sleeping. He slept on the couch. So you can go fuck yourself with your assumptions."

Stella disappears upstairs and I'm left standing there with her suitcases still. My eyes meet Sterling's and he stares back at me blankly.

"What was that about?" I question him, suddenly feeling protective of his fiery sister.

"Nothing that concerns you," he says simply, and I see Olivia scolding him with her expression as she walks past the two of us. "Stella has just had some issues, and we were hoping with her being back home that maybe she can work through them. I'm sorry for assuming you were fucking around with her, I didn't realize she was just sleeping in your bed."

I stare at him, still taken baack by the whole exchange between the two of them. "Yeah, well, maybe you shouldn't just assume shit."

I leave him behind as I turn around and walk up the stairs with Stella's suitcases. They're heavy as fuck and weigh me down, and I feel the strain in my thighs as I climb the staircase.

Somehow, I have a feeling she might have some heavier baggage she's carrying around.

CHAPTER FIVE
STELLA

There's a soft knock on the bedroom door. A sigh slips from my lips and I lift my face from the pillow as I throw daggers with my eyes at whoever is on the other side. I just wanted to be left alone. After having the flight from hell, to having a shit show of a greeting from my lovely brother, I just wanted to go back to sleep and hopefully wake up tomorrow to a better day.

"Come in," I call out, the defeat heavy in my voice.

I watch the knob as it turns slowly and the door is pushed open. Simon stands on the other side with both of my suitcases. I wince, instantly feeling guilty for the way I acted toward him and what he just witnessed. Part of me wants to tell him to leave them and go. But instead, I motion for him to come in.

Simon wheels both suitcases in and I roll over in the bed before sitting up. My legs hang over the edge and Simon stops in front of me, staring down at me with a look of curiosity in his eyes.

"What was that about with your brother?"

A sigh slips from my lips. "Nothing new. I'm sorry for how much of a bitch I was when you picked me up. I've had a hell of a day and I didn't mean to take it out on you."

"It's cool," Simon says simply with a shrug. "I'm not here to be your punching bag, but you can always talk to me about whatever is going on instead of throwing a tantrum."

I stare up at him. "Okay... did you come in here to lecture me too? Would you like to take over my brother's role and monitor me the entire time I'm here?"

"I'm not interested in being like a brother to you, Stella. What would you need to be monitored for anyways?"

"You mean my brother hasn't complained to you about me?" I question him, venom on my tongue. "Shocker."

Simon watches me like he's watching an animal

that is about to attack. I wouldn't blame him if he walked out right now. He has only seen the side I show to the rest of the world. He doesn't know what I've been living up against my entire life.

"As you can imagine, I've always been the fuckup, while Sterling was the golden child," I explain, not sure why I'm telling him my life story like he really cares. "I started drinking in high school and then in college, which is natural. My parents didn't approve of my behavior and the things I was doing. Neither did my brother, which is why he claims I'm fucking up my life. Little does he know, I haven't drank in quite some time and am actually on my own personal journey right now."

Simon tilts his head to the side. "What kind of journey?"

"Self-discovery," I tell him with conviction. "I started college without an idea of what I wanted to do with my life. I know what I want to do now and have declared a major. Now, I'm working on figuring out who I really am. Finding your boyfriend in bed with your best friend will make you reevaluate a lot."

A shadow passes through Simon's expression and he stares at me for a moment. "He did what?"

Shit. I shouldn't have said anything.

"I don't want to talk about it."

Simon's jaw clenches. "Fine." He closes his eyes briefly and lets out a deep breath before changing the subject. "Does anyone really have their life figured out at eighteen?"

"Nineteen," I correct him, scowling as we both ignore the information I just shared. "And probably not, unless your name is Sterling Barrett."

Simon lets out a harsh laugh. "If he led you guys to believe that he had his life figured out, he definitely had you all fooled. Your brother didn't really get his shit together until Olivia came into the picture."

I shake my head, refusing to believe that. "He's always known he wanted to play hockey and that was his lifelong goal. I never had that because it would never come close to touching the pride my parents have for Sterling."

"Okay, first of all," Simon starts as he walks over and drops down onto the bed beside me, "fuck your parents, and I mean that in the nicest way possible. Second, hockey was the only thing Sterling had figured out, and nothing more than that. Third, the only person you should be worried about making proud is yourself."

Falling silent, I stare back at Simon. We've

always had this flirtatious dynamic between us, but this feels much more intimate. Everything has always been at face value and superficial... this is something deeper. And I don't like the emotions it's bringing out inside me.

"Damn, Simon." I quickly swallow back the emotion and raise my eyebrows at him. "Since when did you become such a wise old man?"

His eyebrows pull together and he shakes his head at me. "Don't do that, Stella."

"Do what?" I challenge him, giving him an innocent smile.

"Turn it into some kind of a joke," he says, his voice quiet and slightly distant. There's a look in his eyes and it looks very similar to disappointment. "I'm being serious here and I want you to take what I'm saying seriously."

My stomach sinks at his words. He knows that it's all a facade. How the hell can he know me so well to know when I'm just brushing things off? I have certain coping mechanisms and turning everything into a joke or a lighthearted moment is one of them. I don't do well with my emotions and Simon is trying to resurrect them again.

"I know you're being serious," I admit, my voice barely above a whisper. "I wasn't trying to make it a joke, just trying to make it not such a heavy moment."

Simon falls silent as he stares at me for a second. "What's wrong with heavy? You tired of carrying the weight, baby girl?"

My breath catches in my throat as his words bounce around in my head. Never mind the fact that he called me a new little pet name—but he hit the nail directly on the head. I am tired of carrying the fucking weight. I'm tired of being the black sheep and feeling like I'm a walking, talking disappointment.

It's too heavy and it feels like it's constantly weighing me down.

"Yeah," I whisper, tearing my gaze from his as I drop it down to my hands that are neatly folded in my lap. "Sometimes it just feels like a lot."

"I get that," he says gently. "You don't have to take on the weight of everything. Fuck them all and their assumptions. Let them have their own thoughts and just prove them wrong. You can't control how other people react or the way they think. All you can do is control your own feelings and thoughts."

"I didn't know you had such a good head on your shoulders, Simon," I admit, lifting my gaze back to his. "I thought you were just carefree because you didn't give a shit about anything going on in the world around you. You've done a lot of work to get here, haven't you?"

Now it's Simon's turn to feel as uncomfortable as he just made me feel. I'm laying it all out there and holding back no punches. He wanted to call me out on my shit and bring my feelings to the surface, so I'm doing the same to him. Not necessarily for a reaction, but if I have to face a few of my demons, so does he.

The corners of his lips lift upward as he smiles at me. "Let's just say that I went through a lot of therapy when I was younger. I struggled badly with depression. Thankfully, I was put on medication and got it all straightened out, but to answer your question—yes. I did have to do a lot of internal work and work on my mindset to get where I am now."

I stare at him with the silence settling around us as I'm taken aback by the way he just admitted that with ease, like it doesn't even bother him at all. It's all just fact, part of his story, and he's more than willing to share that part of his journey with me. Although, he does keep it close to his chest and doesn't fully reveal all of his cards. There's something about his past he doesn't want to tell me, and that's okay.

I won't push him for any answers because maybe that shit is too heavy as well.

And Simon doesn't look like someone to let any amount of weight drag him down.

CHAPTER SIX

SIMON

After leaving Stella in her room to take a nap, I went back downstairs. Lincoln was still sitting in the living room watching TV and Olivia and Sterling were getting the last of their things together. I walked into the kitchen, pausing as I watched the two of them conversing together by the fridge.

"You gotta stop being so hard on Stella," I break through their conversation, directing my words at Sterling. "She's trying to work on herself and your negativity isn't really helping."

Sterling slowly turns his head, his eyes landing on mine. And they're fucking ice cold.

"Okay," he says after a moment of silence. There's an iciness to his tone, but for whatever reason, he just simply agrees. "I'll try to go a little easier on her."

I stare back at him, completely caught off guard. "Wait, you're not going to argue with me or tell me to stay out of your family's business?"

Sterling shakes his head and Olivia smiles from beside him. "There's no sense, because you're right. I am hard on her, but that's because I don't want to see her do something really bad and completely fuck up her life. I want better for her, as I always have. I've always felt the need to protect her, but Stella has always tried to show me in any way she could that she doesn't need my protection."

"She just wants to be her own person and to have the freedom to discover who that person is."

Sterling shrugs. "I'm not that worried about her if she's here with you. I know you won't let her get into any trouble."

He's right, I won't let her do anything that is going to have any serious implications, but that is beside the point and Sterling still isn't getting it. I didn't realize his relationship with his sister was this strained. I knew they had their struggles and they fought like normal siblings, but I didn't realize they had issues like this.

"You're right, I won't, but that's not the point,

bro. The point is to not control her. Stella is allowed to fuck up and make mistakes. She's only human and we've all done the same shit. No one can control her and the more you fight against that, the harder she's going to fight back against you."

Olivia tilts her head to the side. "How do you know her so well? Did you get all of this from observing her when she's come to visit over the years?" There's no accusation in Olivia's voice. She's genuinely curious. Probably wondering how I figured out her best friend when she couldn't see the true power struggle going on right in front of her face.

"Because I used to be the same exact way."

I can't help but feel like I'm being judged under Olivia's and Sterling's gazes. I know they really aren't judging me like I feel they are, but instead it's like they're both trying to figure me out. Surprisingly, I worked through the majority of my shit during high school, so when I came to Wyncote, I had my head on straight.

Sterling never saw the messy side of me. I had myself cleaned up and was already four years into working on my mindset when we met. No one in my life now knew the struggles I went through when I was deeply depressed. No one knew about a lot of shit, and I wasn't about to spill all of my secrets to these guys right now.

Sterling is one of my closest friends, but I had a feeling that shit was going to end after tomorrow. He's already moving out today, tomorrow he's graduating, and then who the fuck knows what comes next. He doesn't need to know what I've gone through mentally, but he needs to understand that what he's doing with his sister isn't going to work.

It's only going to push her farther away.

"So, what do you suggest is the best way to handle Stella?" Olivia questions me, speaking for the two of them since Sterling seems to be at a loss for words. "She's always been a little bit of a wild one and I don't know what to do to help her. I feel like I've been watching her spiral down this road of destruction for a while now."

"Did she tell you she hasn't been drinking?" I ask them, to which they both shake their heads at me. "Maybe you can act like you give a shit, even if you don't. Ask her about stuff, even if it might be hard to talk about. And don't push her, because you're just going to lose her if you continue to do that. Let her come forth with stuff on her own time, but still be there to show your support."

"It's not like she was an alcoholic or struggled

with addiction," Sterling tells me with a defensive bite to his tone. "She was just drinking a lot more than she should have been."

"Yeah, which is still an issue," I argue with him. "She was obviously trying to escape something. The alcohol wasn't the root cause of the problem. It was just her solution in the moment."

"What's she doing differently now?" Olivia asks me, like I am Stella's personal fucking representative. And honestly, it's kind of pissing me off now. They're asking me all these questions when they could ask her themselves.

"Why don't you ask her yourself? Have a conversation and get to know the girl you claim is your best friend."

I don't mean to be an asshole to Olivia, especially when she's one of the nicest people I've ever met, but Jesus Christ. Stella is a real live person. I thought she and Olivia were closer than Olivia is making it seem right now. She's acting like Stella is more of a stranger than anything. I know that they've grown apart since they lived across the country from each other, but it's not like they didn't talk all the time.

Sterling is quiet again, like something heavy is weighing on his mind. Instead of questioning him on it, I leave the two of them in the kitchen as I head into the living room. Lincoln glances up at me as I drop down onto the couch, an exasperated sigh slipping from my lips.

"What was that about? I thought you and Sterling were, like, best friends?"

I glance over at him and shrug. "I don't know, man. After seeing the way he's so quick to snap at his little sister, I'm not so sure what to make of him anymore. I don't know their entire history, so who am I to really judge?"

"She's lucky to have you on her side," Lincoln says quietly as he directs his gaze back to the TV. My eyes follow his and I stare absentmindedly at the screen as it goes out of focus.

I don't know where the sense of needing to protect her has come from, but I've already made up my mind. If Stella needs me to go up to bat for her, I will.

Even if it's against her own brother.

CHAPTER SEVEN
STELLA

The sun is hot as it hangs above in the sky. It's the middle of the afternoon and it's beginning to get really warm outside. That's one thing I love about Vermont summers. The winters may be brutal, but the weather during the summer months is truly enjoyable. It gets hot, but not like it does out west. It's definitely a different kind of heat and I didn't realize how much I missed it while I was gone.

Today is the day my brother graduates college. Even though we have our differences, I'm still excited and happy for him. Next month, he should hopefully be getting drafted into the NHL. He has so many big things coming up in life, I can't help but feel a sense of pride for him.

But at the same time, I'm more relieved than anything. With him graduating, that means I won't have to see him very often. He'll be too preoccupied with what is going on in his life to worry about what I'm doing with mine. I really took Simon's words to heart. I want to prove everyone who has doubted me wrong.

Even my English teacher from my senior year of high school. That asshole told me that I would never amount to anything in life if I continued the way I was. Which was probably a fair statement... but it's one I will never forget and have carried with me this long.

I'll prove them all wrong.

Sitting in the stands, Olivia is on one side of me while Simon is on the other, and my parents are sitting in the row behind the three of us. They had said they would be here, so that meant they were coming and nothing was going to stop them. After all, their golden child is graduating college today.

I hate the way I feel so much animosity because of it. My brother and I have always had our struggles, but shouldn't we be coming closer together as we are in adulthood now? Aren't we supposed to be friends and enjoy life instead of constantly fighting still?

Maybe it really comes down to me and my mindset. I've had such a chip on my shoulder toward him because of feeling like I was beneath him. If I would just change my thoughts and attitude toward him, maybe that would make a world of difference. He would read my energy and match it, instead of throwing negativity right back at me.

Life and my relationships in it don't have to be as hard as I've made them in the past.

"I'm so glad you're here, sweetie," my mother says from behind me as she puts her hands on my shoulders. Her touch makes me rigid for a moment, but I brush the irritation away. Lifting my hand, I put it over hers and turn my head to look at her with a smile.

"I wouldn't miss it for the world," I tell her with nothing but honesty. Even though we've all had our differences and struggles, I wouldn't miss this moment for my brother. And all of the other ones to come that are worth celebrating. I will always be supportive of him, regardless of my own feelings.

Releasing my mother's hand, I turn back around and we're all staring at the stage. Simon claps for his friends and teammates as they walk across the stage when each of their names are called. Sterling is one of the first, so we all jump to our feet, clapping and hooting and hollering.

Olivia looks like she's prouder than my goddamn parents. There's nothing but love in my best friend's eyes and I can't even be mad. When I first found out about her and my brother, I was definitely pissed, but I didn't let it show. How could I do that? I didn't want to be the one to tarnish her happiness. Even though I felt like I deserved to feel it, that doesn't mean I wanted to shit all over everyone else's happiness.

My brother looks over at all of us, throwing his hand in the air in celebration. It isn't often that his grumpy ass smiles, but his face lights up like he's on top of the universe right now. A soft chuckle falls from my lips and I feel Simon's eyes on the side of my face as we sit down.

I turn to look at him, my lips parted slightly as the smile settles on my face.

"I like you like this," Simon says quietly, his eyes bouncing back and forth between mine. "Happiness looks good on you, baby girl."

There it is again. My breath catches in my throat and my stomach does a flip as those two little words play over and over in my head. There's something about the way he says it, the way it sounds rolling off his tongue. I've never wanted to taste something this badly before.

"I'm trying," I admit, smiling at him. "Changing your thought process isn't the easiest thing."

"It isn't but I promise you it does get easier until you don't even really have to think about it." He smiles and winks at me.

He shocks me again, reaching over as he grabs my hand and lightly squeezes it. "I'm cheering for you, Stella. I believe in you."

"I don't understand why," I admit, my voice soft and quiet, feeling his absence as he pulls his hand away from mine. "You know me from the time I've come to visit, that's really it. You're more friends with my brother, so why would you believe in me?"

Simon shrugs, a crooked grin still fixed on his lips. "Because I can tell you really want it. There's something about you, Stella..."

I wait for him to continue, but he doesn't. Instead, he lets his unfinished sentence hang in the air as he turns his head to look back up at the stage. I've never been a fan of cliffhangers, and this might be the worst one I've ever experienced. It felt like there was a but or some kind of an explanation coming after his words.

But there was nothing more he was going to give me.

I am going to have to make my own interpretation of it and if I let my mind go too wild with it, I might end up falling off that damn cliff he set me up on.

And if I fall, I don't know what comes after that.

CHAPTER EIGHT
SIMON

After the graduation ceremony, everyone split up to go get dinner and celebrate with their families. We planned a huge party at our house tonight. Since most of the other guys are already practically wifed up and have their own places, ours felt like the perfect one to have a party at. It's big enough to fit the amount of people that were invited, and I can't even tell you who everyone on the list is.

Stella and Sterling both went out to dinner with their parents and Olivia went along with them. I was invited along but felt like I was imposing in a way. It wasn't really my place to attend, even though I've been living with Sterling for the past two years.

Lincoln and I headed back to our house to get

everything ready. After we stopped and picked up a few kegs, along with some bottles of liquor, we went back to set up. We decided to forgo on any decorations, because if we're being real here, no one gives a shit about any of that.

Instead, we set up two different tables for beer pong and set up the kegs out back. Our backyard isn't very big but we have a pretty decent-sized patio for people to hang out on. Lincoln insisted on setting up some corn hole out back too, so I didn't bother to argue with him. It was his house too and he was just as excited to celebrate our friends' accomplishments.

Lincoln and I end up on the couch, playing video games, while we wait for everyone to show up. About two hours after parting ways following the graduation ceremony, everyone begins to show up. The first ones to show are Isla and Logan. August and Poppy aren't far behind them, along with Hayden and Eden.

I stand up as they begin to file into the house, hugging all of my brothers and their girls. August is the last one that I pull in for a hug and I take a step back, looking back and forth between him and Poppy.

"Where's Ev at tonight?" I ask the two of them.

Poppy raises an eyebrow at me. "Surely you didn't think we would be bringing a baby to the party... right?"

"He's with Poppy's parents for the night," August chimes in as laughter falls from my lips.

"I mean, he is a part of the family, but I don't think this is the best environment for him tonight." I shake my head at Poppy and she laughs along with me.

"As much as I love having the kid, I'm ready for a night that we don't have to worry about any responsibilities," August admits as he pulls Poppy flush against his side. "I'm trying to get you home tonight and not have to worry about any interruptions."

Isla makes a gagging sound from where she's standing with Logan. "I don't need that visual in my head, thanks."

Logan and August both share a look before laughing.

"I mean, it's not like your brother didn't hear you fucking his best friend when the three of you lived together," Hayden offers with an arrogant smirk.

Eden slaps his arm. "Hayden King."

He glances at her with a look of innocence. "What? I'm just being real here."

"You're impossible," she mutters, shaking her head as she fights the grin that pulls on her lips. She directs her attention to me. "Where's the liquor? I need something strong to put up with Hayden's antics tonight."

"Hey, you know you love me," he tells her with a wink.

"I do," she admits, smiling up at him. "But when you're around your boys, you're something else. I don't know if this house is big enough for you and your ego."

Hayden gasps, slapping a hand over his chest. "You wound me, baby."

Eden winks at him. "I'll lick your wounds later."

"So, about that liquor," I break through their conversation, feeling like I'm imposing on each and every one of them right now. Lincoln and I are the only two here that are single and I'm slightly envious.

Eden looks over to me, smiling before she follows me into the kitchen where I have everything spread out on the counter. I grab a cup and mix her a drink as I hear Asher and his girlfriend, Sydney, walk into the house with Cam and his girl, Aspen.

After handing Eden her cup, I head back out into the living room to greet the rest of my friends. It feels like old times, having everyone here. And at the same time, it kind of sucks thinking about this being our last night together. Everyone's lives have changed so much over the years and this is literally our last hoorah before everyone goes their separate ways.

Some other people that graduated with them or went to Wyncote end up coming in until we have practically a full house. Sterling, Olivia, and Stella are the last ones to show up. By the time they get to the house, I'm already two beers deep and have won one round of beer pong with Hayden.

I abandon the table and Eden takes my place as I head directly to Stella. She's hovering near the couch, her eyes trailing around the room as she takes in the entire party that is already in full swing. There isn't anything uncomfortable about her stance. Instead, it looks like she's just surveying the area, almost like she's people watching.

"Hey you," I say quietly as I approach her. She lifts her gaze to mine, her bright eyes shining back at me. "How was dinner?"

She purses her lips and shrugs. "It could have been worse. My parents seemed pretty happy to see me and to hear that I finally declared a major. I told them I'm not drinking anymore, but I don't know if they fully believed me."

My heart hurts for her. I know that Stella has really been trying hard. Even though I haven't personally witnessed it, I believe her. I don't think she would really lie to me about it. What could she possibly have to gain? In the grand scheme of things, I'm not really anyone that makes a difference in her life. I'm just simply here to show my support as someone who has experienced similar struggles.

"You told them the truth. What they decide to do with that is completely up to them. All of that is beyond your control now, so there's no point in letting it bother you or even entertaining the thoughts that enter your mind."

Stella stares back at me, her eyes searching mine. "You know, I really appreciate you, Simon," she says, her voice soft and gentle, feeling like silk as it slides through my ears. "I haven't really had much support from anyone else, but you seem to know the right things to say at the exact times I need to hear them."

"That's what I'm here for, baby girl." The corners of my lips lift into a grin and I wink at her. "We all need someone to be on our side."

Her lips mirror mine as they break out into a grin and she flashes her white teeth at me. "It looks like this is going to be quite the party tonight." She pauses, glancing down at the bottle of beer in my hand. "What are you drinking?"

I lift it up to show her. "Some IPA your brother had in the fridge." Falling silent, I mentally want to kick myself for not even thinking about her not drinking. "Shit. Is it going to bother you, being around alcohol?"

A soft laugh falls from her lips. "I'm not an alcoholic, Simon," she says, shaking her head at me. "I was just drinking too much. It was never to the point where I felt like I needed it or had to drink. There's literally no temptation there, so no, it doesn't bother me being around it. I honestly don't even want to drink at all."

Her words bring me some reassurance that this isn't going to be a bad situation for her.

"I'm glad. I didn't even think about you being at a party where everyone is drinking."

Stella smiles at me. "I don't need to drink to have fun, Simon."

"Good to know," I tell her, holding my hand out to her. "Come on. Let's go get on the list for the beer pong table. I want to kick Hayden's ass from all the shit he's constantly talking."

Stella's palm is warm as she slides it against

mine, lacing her fingers through my own. "Let's go kick his ass and knock him down a peg or two."

———

Three games later, we didn't manage to beat Hayden and Eden. The two of them are practically unstoppable. They've been running the table and loving every minute of it. And Eden is literally exactly like Hayden with the way she gets cocky and runs her mouth.

Seriously, he couldn't have found a better girl.

Stella and I end up on the couch where some people are sitting and talking. Most of the guys are scattered throughout the room. August and Poppy have already left. It isn't often that they get time alone from the baby, so I can't say I blame them for leaving early for some alone time together.

It's still loud with the music pumping through the speakers and everyone partying hard. After finishing the beer I had in my hand when Stella got here, I haven't had another one since. There's something about being around her and the fact that she isn't drinking that makes me not want to as well. I want to have fun without having any alcohol involved.

"Aren't you drinking anymore?" Stella asks me, her thigh pressed against mine. I inhale deeply, smelling her sweet scent that smells like berries.

I shake my head at her, leaning closer because of how loud the music is. "Nope. I stopped drinking earlier."

Her eyebrows tug together slightly. "Why?"

"Because I didn't want you to be the only one not drinking."

She stares at me and her eyes briefly search mine. "You didn't have to do that, Simon. I'm completely fine with being the only sober one here."

Turning my head to the side, I lean toward her, my lips just barely brushing against her ear. "What if I wanted to be sober with you?"

Lingering for a moment, I hear the sharp intake of her breath before I pull away. There's a fire burning deep inside her eyes as they burn holes through my own. I'm captivated and breathless from the way she's looking at me right now. Like she isn't staring through me... she's looking directly at me, directly into the depths of my soul.

"You want to go upstairs where it's quieter?" she questions me, her voice barely audible over the noise in the room.

A ghost of a smile plays on my lips. Without

saying a word, I rise to my feet and offer my hand down to her. Stella slides her delicate hand into my own, letting me help her up before lacing her fingers through mine.

We walk around the couch and through the living room as we head toward the stairs. My eyes catch Hayden's from across the room and I don't miss the smirk that forms on his face. Just as we're about to walk through the doorway, I see Sterling walking from the kitchen. His gaze meets mine before dropping down to his sister's hand in mine.

I pause for a beat and Stella stops beside me, glancing up at me with a confused look on her face. I look back to where Sterling was standing, but he isn't there any longer. I know how it must have looked to him, but if he had an issue, he would have approached me about it. He wouldn't have let this go any further, even if we are just going upstairs to talk.

Smiling down at Stella, I wink before I begin to lead her upstairs. We bypass Sterling's room that she'll be occupying for the rest of the summer and head directly to mine instead. We step inside and I let go of her hand as she walks past me, dropping down onto my bed. Softly closing the door behind me, I take a deep breath and turn around.

Stella's gaze collides with mine and the flames in her eyes burn brighter. I take a step forward, closing the distance between us, but I stop as I reach the middle of the room. We came up here to talk, but there's a shift in the air and I don't know what I'm supposed to do about it.

I watch her as she stands back up and walks directly toward me, not stopping until her toes reach mine. Tilting my head down to look at her, she tips hers back as she wraps her arms around the back of my neck, so our bodies are pressed flush against one another's.

"Stella." My voice is hoarse and thick with lust as she lifts up onto her toes, her lips just barely brushing against mine. "What are you doing, baby girl?"

"I don't know," she murmurs, nipping at my bottom lip. "There's just something about you..."

CHAPTER NINE
STELLA

Simon pulls back slightly, his eyes bouncing back and forth between mine. The corners of his lips twitch before they crash into mine. The tension between the two of us has been building for quite some time with the way we've always flirted with each other, but this is the first time either of us have ever made a move.

There's a part of me that wonders if we shouldn't be doing this. There's a party in full swing downstairs. Even though some of the people have already left, I know my brother and my best friend are downstairs. And I'm not sure how my brother would feel about this.

Simon's lips are soft against mine and he tastes

like the beer he was drinking earlier. He nips at my bottom lip before sliding his tongue along the seam of mine. I part them, allowing him access inside. His tongue slides across mine before we are caught in a dance of our own.

His hands grip my waist, his fingertips digging into my flesh as he holds me flush against his firm body. My arms are wrapped around the back of his neck and I slide my hands through his now longer hair, feeling the silkiness between my fingertips. What starts out as a gentle kiss quickly becomes something completely different.

He releases my waist and slides one arm around the small of my back as he holds me tightly against him. The other finds the side of my face before he slides his fingers through my hair and wraps the strands around his hand in a fist. His grip is tight on my hair and he pulls my head back slightly as he takes everything from me.

Simon drains the air from my lungs as his lips become more urgent and the kiss deepens. He bruises my lips with his own and I let him, reveling in the pain as he takes what he wants from me. We've been playing this little game of cat and mouse, but now he has me exactly where he wants me. And I was the first one to make the move.

I know he had been holding back out of respect for my brother. That, and the fact that I had a boyfriend all of the times I've stayed here before. I push the thoughts from my mind and allow myself to get completely lost in him and his touch.

He urges me backward, pushing me back until my legs are bumping into the edge of the bed. Abandoning my hair, both of his hands are on my hips and he's lowering me down onto the mattress as he follows along with me. Fully clothed, he settles between my legs and his mouth never leaves mine.

It's like our lips are melting into one another's and our surroundings completely vanish. His hands are sliding my shirt up, his fingertips light as they dance across my skin. I don't stop him because I want this just as badly as he does.

My hands are in his hair and his mouth abandons mine as he traces his tongue along the underside of my jaw. A moan falls from my lips, my eyelids fluttering as he begins his descent down my neck. His lips are sucking and tasting every inch of my skin as they begin to trail down the side of my neck.

Simon pushes my shirt up above my breasts and he slides his hands under my bra, pushing that up with my shirt. I don't know how things are moving so fast but I'm not about to stop him. His cock is hard and I can feel it pressing against my center through our clothes. Removing my hands from his hair, I grip his broad shoulders as he brings his mouth down to my breasts.

He cups one in his palm, then plays with my nipple with his fingers. Rolling it in between his thumb and forefinger, he repeats the motion, alternating as he tugs on it gently. His mouth finds my other nipple, sucking it between his teeth. His tongue is soft against my skin as he rolls it around my nipple.

Lifting his head, his eyes meet mine and there's a fire burning deep in his irises. He lowers his head once more, switching to my other breast as he begins his slow assault on my other nipple, giving it the same attention the first one got.

I'm a mess underneath him, withering under his touch. Lifting my hips, I wrap my legs around his torso, feeling his cock pressing against my pussy. I shift myself, rolling my hips as I search for the friction that my body is craving. Moving against him, his cock rolls against my clit through our clothes.

It's like we're in fucking high school, practically dry fucking each other through our clothes right now. My hands abandon his shoulders and I'm sliding them down his torso until I reach the waist-band of his sweatpants. A groan slips from his lips and I can feel the sound vibrating against my flesh as I slide my fingers underneath the elastic band.

He pulls away from my breasts and rests his forehead against my sternum, a ragged breath slipping from him. His gaze meets mine and I'm lost in the fire again as he stares up at me. "Goddamn, Stella. You're driving me insane right now."

"Good," I smile back at him, "because I want you, Simon. So badly."

A smirk tugs on his lips. "You going to let me taste that pretty pussy, baby girl?"

Pulling my bottom lip in between my teeth, I bite down on my flesh and nod.

Simon begins to move down my torso, his hands finding the top of my pants. He begins to drag them down, pulling my panties with them before he pauses. He strips them away from my body before tossing them onto the floor. Simon settles on his knees and slides his hands under my ass as he pulls me to the edge of the bed.

He settles himself between my legs, his mouth so close to my pussy that I can feel the warmth of his breath against my skin as he breathes out. "I want to hear you say it. Tell me what you want me to do to you, pretty girl."

I swallow roughly, feeling the warmth spreading through my body as I'm craving his touch. "I want you to taste me, Simon."

He shakes his head. "Not good enough, Stella. Tell me what you want."

Fuck.

There's something dominating about him that has me feeling like I'm already soaked. I've never had someone talk to me like this before. Usually, they just took what they wanted or went down on me without needing my instructions. Simon is demanding this from me and it has me on the spot right now.

"I want you to eat my pussy," I murmur, my voice hoarse and thick with need. "I don't want you to stop until you make me come."

A look of approval passes through his expression and there's a storm brewing in his metallic-colored eyes as he nods. "Good girl. You tell me what you want and you'll be rewarded."

His breath is hot against my pussy and I almost come completely undone as he slides his tongue along my center. He starts at the bottom, licking his way to the top before circling his tongue around my clit. A moan slips from my lips and I don't bother trying to swallow back the sounds.

He doesn't stop at just that. He's skilled with his wicked tongue as he licks me up and down, each time teasing my clit when he reaches the top. That's what I want. I want him to play with it until I'm shattering into a million pieces. And it's as if he knows it. Instead of focusing just on that, he's fucking teasing me and it's driving me wild.

Simon parts my legs farther until I'm practically in a split. He plants his forearms against my thighs, pinning them to the bed as I try to wiggle underneath him. My hands find his hair and I'm gripping his locks tightly against his scalp. My hips buck, but he doesn't let me move as he continues his slow assault against my pussy.

It's driving me absolutely insane and I don't know how much longer I can take it. I just want him to focus on my clit and he is purposely bypassing it. A groan of frustration escapes me.

"Oh my god, Simon," I murmur, my voice cracking around my words. "Stop fucking teasing me and show me how well you can fuck me with that mouth."

Simon pulls his face away from me, his eyes

finding mine. A shadow passes over his face. "You think I'm not doing a good job already?"

I narrow my eyes at him, the warmth building in the pit of my stomach. "You know what you're doing. Stop fucking around and make me come."

He removes his right arm from my thigh and lightly slaps my pussy. It stings my flesh but at the same time it sends a streak of electricity through my body, making my nerves feel like they're on fire. I let out a yelp, the pain mixing with pleasure.

My chest is rising and falling in rapid succession as my breathing grows ragged. My heart pounds erratically in my chest and it feels like it could burst through my rib cage at any moment.

"What was that for?" I practically pant, my voice needy because I kind of want him to do it again.

"You told me what you wanted, so I felt you needed to feel a different type of reward." Simon tilts his head to the side, his tongue darting out of his mouth as he licks me from top to bottom before looking up at me again. "Are you implying you didn't like it? Because I saw the way your body reacted to it."

I swallow roughly, not wanting to admit that I actually did like it. "So, what if I did?"

"That's what I thought." He smirks before diving

back into my pussy. He works his mouth against me, eating me like a starved man. I swear to God, he's going to completely consume me.

And then there's a knock on the door. Simon quickly lifts his head, our gazes colliding in an instant. My eyes are wide and I'm abruptly sitting up on the bed.

"Stella?" I hear Olivia's voice from the other side of the door. "Are you in there?"

Fuck. Fuck. Fuck.

I'm still staring at Simon. "What the hell do I do?"

"Just chill the fuck out and tell her you'll be out in a minute."

Jesus Christ. How could I have been so stupid to think that no one would come up here looking for me?

"Yeah, I am," I call out to her as I practically jump to my feet. Simon hands me my underwear and pants and I quickly pull them on. "Simon and I were just talking. I'll be right out."

After adjusting my pants and panties, I realize that my bra and shirt are still pushed up high on my chest. I quickly pull both of them back into place. As I turn around, I see that Simon is sitting on his bed, looking completely unfazed by the whole thing.

"How are you so calm right now?"

He shrugs. "Because I don't give a shit if anyone knows about this. Why are you so worked up about it? We came up to my room to talk—do you think that anyone is going to actually buy that?"

"I don't know. Shit, I don't fucking know. This wasn't supposed to happen."

Simon's eyebrows draw together and a pained look washes over his expression. "Why is that?"

"Because you're my brother's roommate. I'm supposed to be on my journey to self-discovery and that doesn't involve falling into bed with someone else."

"I think you should look at it differently, maybe from a more positive perspective," Simon offers, his voice gentle. "You're discovering things about yourself where there are no attachments involved. I'm not asking for anything from you, Stella. But maybe this can help you figure out and explore some things you didn't know about yourself before."

I stare at him as I let his words float around in my mind before absorbing them. He has a point, but Olivia is still on the other side of the door waiting for me. "We're not done here, but we'll talk about this tomorrow."

Leaving Simon where he's sitting, I quickly slip

out of his bedroom and pull the door shut behind me. Olivia is standing across the hall, a patient and kind look on her face. She smiles at me, giving me a knowing look without even saying anything.

"Just don't," I tell her, shaking my head as a nervous laugh slips from my lips.

"I wasn't going to." She smiles at me before giving me a wink. "I just wanted to come say bye to you before we head out. I want to get together soon so we can have some girl time."

"Of course." I smile back at her, pulling her in for a hug. "Call me tomorrow?"

"You got it," she nods as she steps away from me. "And enjoy the rest of your night," she adds with another wink.

I shake my head and fall into step with her as we begin to walk down the hall. "I'm taking my ass to bed before I do something stupid."

Olivia doesn't say anything about my remark, but instead just says goodnight to me before she disappears downstairs. I slip into my new bedroom and immediately flop down onto the bed. I'm on my back, staring up at the ceiling as I think about the events that happened tonight.

My body is still humming from Simon's touch and I'm craving the feeling of his tongue between my legs. I wasn't ready for it to be over, but maybe it was best that Olivia interrupted us.

I need to figure out what the hell I want before I end up in bed with Simon Murray again.

Maybe he can be a part of my journey... just as long as he doesn't become my destination.

CHAPTER TEN
SIMON

The next morning as I walk down into the living room, I see no signs of Stella anywhere. Her bedroom door was closed when I walked past, but I didn't bother to stop and check in on her. After last night, I'm not sure that she really wants to see me. Although, I do have some lasting hope.

She may have played it off like this was all a bad idea, especially with her being on her own path of self-discovery, but she also seemed a little open to exploring other things along her journey. And I'm literally just along for the ride right now.

I have one more year left of being tied down to Wyncote University and then I'm off to do my own thing. Hopefully following in the footsteps of my friends and playing professionally. It's hard to say that it will actually happen. Playing in the NHL is every hockey player's dream, but the odds are stacked against us.

The percentage of people who actually make it onto a professional team is extraordinarily low. Considering the fact that most players play until they're in their forties, it's not like new positions are opening up on teams constantly.

I try not to think about the negatives and just focus on what my main goal is. And if it doesn't happen, there's always other options. There's the AHL and then there are different coaching opportunities. The list is literally endless, but there's one specific goal that sits at the very top of my list and I didn't work this fucking hard to not get a shot at it.

With that being said, I'm not looking for a relationship or getting involved with anyone on a level like that. And thankfully, Stella is on the same page. Although, it seems like she might not want to be involved with anyone in any way, but last night was a little bit contradictory to what she was saying a few moments before that.

Only time will tell what actually happens. There's a part of me that is regretting the camp I signed up for in Canada right now. I leave in less than a week to go to that and it lasts almost a month. After last night with Stella, I was looking forward to some extra time with her, but it looks like that might get cut short now.

I walk into the kitchen and begin to make something for breakfast when Lincoln comes strolling in. Lifting my gaze away from the stove, I tilt my head to the side, taking in his disheveled appearance. His hair is a complete mess and he's not wearing a shirt, which showcases the ink that's sprawled across his skin.

Glancing behind him, I don't miss the whirlwind of some girl sneaking out through the front door. Lincoln sighs, running a hand through his tangled hair as our gazes collide. I raise an eyebrow at him in question and he shrugs.

"Last night was a rough one. You disappeared early... you and Stella," he adds with a smirk as he moves his eyebrows up and down.

I return his shrug. "We went upstairs to talk and then I ended up just going to bed. Wasn't really in the mood for all of the commotion down here."

"Mhm," Lincoln murmurs as he reaches the fridge and grabs a bottle of water from inside it. "Call it whatever you want. You missed out on one hell of a party, though."

"Yeah, I'm sure," I play along, turning back to the stove as I flip the pancakes I'm in the middle of cooking. Lincoln has been to some of the parties we've all been to, but this is still his first year of college. I've had my fair share of parties and, to be honest, I don't really care about them like I used to. "Who was the girl sneaking out?"

Lincoln laughs lightly. "That's a good question. I didn't get her name… or if I did, I honestly don't remember what it was."

"Just be careful, bro," I tell him, shaking my head as I glance over at him. "I lived the life you did and I get it, trust me I do. But shit can also go sideways faster than you expect it to."

Lincoln shrugs and he reminds me a fucking lot of Hayden King. "I'll deal with the problems as they come."

Hayden King had the same exact attitude when he came here, although I think it's safe to say that he was a little cockier. He had gotten himself into some trouble at the last university he attended before transferring to Wyncote, which isn't the case with Lincoln.

I don't know that I would even consider Lincoln a playboy, necessarily. Definitely a fuckboy, though. We all have similarities when it comes to how we shy away from relationships and focus mainly on hockey. Lincoln is a little different, though. He's completely detached from having any type of romantic feelings, but his bedroom door is definitely a revolving one, with different girls in and out on the regular.

"Well, don't you look chipper this morning," I hear Lincoln's voice from the dining room area.

"You'll learn quickly that I'm not much of a morning person," Stella's voice sounds from the direction Lincoln is in. My heart picks up its pace in my chest as the sound of her singsong voice plays against my eardrums like a sweet melody.

"Neither am I, babe, but I can promise you that I'm a night owl for sure."

"Nice try," Stella laughs at him, her voice getting closer as she heads toward my direction. "You're not my type and I'm not looking to get involved with anyone."

"How am I not your type?" Lincoln calls after her. "I can be whatever you want me to be. I'm everyone's type, babe."

Stella walks into the room and our gazes collide. She lets out an exasperated sigh as she rolls her eyes. Lincoln isn't far behind her, a playful smirk playing on his lips. He knows better after Sterling's warning, but he wouldn't be himself if he didn't try to come on to her and test the limits.

I look past her, my eyes meeting Lincoln's as I narrow mine at him. My jaw clenches and I can't help but feel a sense of annoyance toward him at this moment. Stella isn't mine, but I was the one who was between her legs last night with the taste of her sweet pussy on my tongue.

"She's off-limits, Reid," I remind him, the ice in my tone slicing through his flesh. Lincoln tilts his head to the side and a knowing look passes through his eyes. He knows that Stella was in my room last night. He knows that Sterling warned him to keep his distance. He knows that he's in the fucking wrong right now and he better tread lightly.

"I'm just fucking around," he admits, shrugging as a chuckle vibrates in his chest. He directs his gaze back to Stella. "I'm sorry and I wasn't trying to be disrespectful at all. It was all just good fun and I apologize for being an asshole."

"It's cool," Stella tells him with a simple shrug. "I grew up with an older brother, it's not like I didn't have his dickhead friends try to come on to me, not to mention the other assholes I went to school with. I get it all being fun, but we don't have to do it this way. And trust me, Lincoln. I have no problem in crushing you like a little fucking bug beneath my shoe. So, don't push me in that direction, especially since we're going to be sharing an apartment for the next few months."

Lincoln's eyes widen slightly and I fight back the laughter that bubbles in my chest. I love the fiery side of Stella Barrett. The one that isn't afraid to tell you to go get fucked. She doesn't need anyone to protect her or to keep her safe. Stella is entirely capable of holding her own and making sure no one fucks with her.

She's stronger and more independent than she gives herself credit for. She has this fucked-up perception that her brother is better than her and what she's doing doesn't amount to him playing hockey. Stella has no idea and it hurts my heart at how she views herself as insignificant compared to him.

"Shit, I like her," Lincoln mumbles to me, winking before he disappears from the kitchen, leaving Stella and I alone.

My eyes trail along her body, looking her up and down as I take in her comfortable appearance. She looks beautiful, her face free from any makeup and her hair pulled up in a messy bun on top of her head. I love the way she looks in the pair of black sweatpants she's wearing. My eyes travel across the graphic words on her white t-shirt and I can't help but smile.

"Fuck you, you fucking fuck?" I question her, raising my eyebrow as I read the words out loud.

Stella smiles at me and it reaches her eyes. It's brighter than the sun that hangs in the sky and it melts my heart on the spot. I can't be letting myself feel these things when it comes to her, but goddamn, it's nearly impossible to fight the way she makes my stomach flutter when she smiles at me like that.

"Yep," she flashes her bright white teeth and nods. I watch her as she backs up to the counter, planting her hands on the marble before she lifts herself up to sit on it. "It's from *Shameless*. If you even tell me you've never seen that show, we most definitely cannot be friends."

I smile back at her. "Of course, I've seen that show. What, do you think I've been living under a rock?"

Stella tilts her head to the side, her eyes traveling up and down the length of my body before she pulls her bottom lip between her teeth. "Hmm. I don't know. It's hard to tell. I don't know that I would say you've been living under a rock, but definitely with your head up your own ass."

"Ouch," I fake a wince, pressing my hand to my chest over my heart. "You wound me, Stella. Thinking so little of me like that."

"Let's be real, Simon." She rolls her eyes, a playfulness in her tone. "I think I know you well enough now to know what you're about. You might not have your head up your own ass, but you're definitely only concerned with what you have going on in life."

"I think I liked it better when you said that my head was up my ass."

Stella shrugs. "Okay, maybe both are harsh accusations. But tell me, Simon... when was the last time you cared about what was going on in someone else's life but your own?"

The moment that you walked into my life.

"I'm not like your brother," I tell her, knowing that is exactly what she's hinting at. Her brother has a one-track mind and even though Olivia might be in his sights now, other than her, he isn't really concerned about anyone but himself. And I'm not saying that as a bad thing or a fault. That's just what Stella is used to, so it's only natural she would assume that her brother's friend is the exact same way. "Believe it or not, I give a shit about people and concern myself with what is going on in their lives."

Stella falls silent as she stares back at me for a moment, like she's seriously considering my words. She doesn't say a word, but the look in her eyes is a thoughtful one as she nods. "Prove it."

Tilting my head to the side, my eyebrows tug together. "Prove what?"

"That you're not like my brother."

I stare back at her, this time finding myself being the one who's caught off guard and silent. "How am I supposed to do that?"

Stella pushes off the counter, landing on her feet with grace and balance. A smirk tugs on the corner of her lips and she shrugs as she spins on her heel to head out of the room. "You'll figure it out."

She disappears from the room and my lips part slightly as I stare through the doorway she just slipped through. She wants me to prove that I'm nothing like her brother...

Challenge accepted.

CHAPTER ELEVEN
STELLA

It's later in the afternoon and I haven't seen Simon since this morning. I don't know where he ended up going, but I heard the engine of his car when he pulled out of the driveway around noon. It wasn't my business, I wasn't his keeper, so I didn't bother asking him. I was surprised to find the house empty, though, when I eventually made my way back downstairs.

Lincoln must have gone with him, so it left me here alone. It felt strange in a way. This was my brother's home for the past four years, the one I visited him at and stayed with him whenever I was in town. Yet, it didn't feel like it was my home. I can't quite put it into words, but I think it has to do with the internal work I'm trying to sift through.

I'm not quite sure where I really belong.

California didn't feel like home and neither does here.

Olivia called me after I got a shower when I realized the boys weren't here anymore. She's stopping by to pick me up to go get mani-pedis since she and Sterling are leaving tomorrow. Their moving date got pushed up a few days sooner, so this is the only girl time we are really going to get and I need to take advantage of that.

What am I going to do without my best friend all summer?

Who is going to interrupt me when I find myself giving in to the temptation of Simon?

She's at the house promptly at two in the afternoon, which is typical of Olivia. She's always been the predictable, safe one. So when she says that she's going to be somewhere at a certain time, you better damn well believe her. I don't know if she's ever been late to anything in her entire life.

As I climb into her car, Olivia looks over at me with a sad smile. "I can't believe this is the last time we get to hang out for who knows how long."

"Is there something you're not telling me? Because you're starting to act like you're going to be leaving me forever."

Olivia puts the car back in drive as I put on my seat belt and she backs out of the driveway. I half expected her to show up in Sterling's car, but she must have gotten hers from her parents' house. That is one thing I still need to figure out—my car from high school is still at my parents', so maybe I could get Olivia to drop me off there afterward to get it.

"I'm not leaving you forever, but I made a decision and I don't want you to be mad at me."

I look over at her, tilting my head to the side as she glances at me from the corner of her eye. "What is it?"

Olivia lets out a deep breath. "I've decided to move wherever Sterling ends up. If he gets drafted, I'm going to transfer schools and move with him."

I stare at her, my lips parted slightly. "I would never be mad at you for that, Liv," I tell her with nothing but honesty in my words. "I want you to be happy and he's what makes you happy. I just don't want you to regret following after him. But I fully support whatever you want to do."

She pulls the car up to a stoplight and looks over at me, her eyes wet as a smile pulls on the corners of her lips. "You really mean that? I hate leaving when you just got here, but I really do love him, Stella.

He's the only one I can imagine my future with and I'm willing to make whatever sacrifices I have to."

"You act like I can't drive or get on a plane." I smile at her, laughing lightly. "We can still visit each other. It will basically just be like when I was in California and you moved here. Our friendship can withstand anything, regardless of the distance."

"You know I love you, girl," Olivia winks at me, her smile bright as the light turns green and she begins to drive the car again.

"Best friends forever," I tell her, holding my hand out to her.

She slides hers into mine. "Always."

———

After getting our mani-pedis, we end up at a cute little restaurant down the block that just so happens to have mimosas all day long and they never card anyone. Olivia has never been a big drinker, but she agreed to have at least one to celebrate the big things coming in her life with Sterling. Surprisingly, one turned into three and with how much of a lightweight Olivia is, she's well past tipsy.

I limited myself to one, because I'm not going back to that darker part of my life. I'm able to have one drink and not get drunk and be able to cut myself off. Olivia was the one who decided to order herself two more and she didn't push me when I turned the offer down. I don't need that to enjoy myself anymore. I also wasn't going to be the one who held her back from letting loose.

I am just enjoying spending the time with my best friend, which we haven't been able to have in so long.

"I know we'll still get to see each other periodically, but I'm really going to miss you," I admit, my voice thick with emotion that I absolutely hate. The last thing I want to do is cry about this. We've spent a lot more time apart, but there is a part of me that was hoping to see her more this summer since we were both supposed to be in Vermont.

I was wrong and I can't help but feel a little disappointed about it. It's a contradiction, though, because at the same time, I feel an overwhelming sense of happiness and I'm proud of her. Olivia found her place in the world where I'm still feeling fucking lost.

"I'm going to miss you too," Olivia slurs her words slightly as she gives me a crooked smile. "Man, those mimosas are really starting to catch up to me. I think," she giggles, "I think I might want to get another one."

"Girl, I know you've only had three, but I think I need to cut you off," I tell her, laughing along with her. "My brother isn't going to be too happy if you get completely shit-faced, and I'm going to be the one to blame for it."

Olivia's eyebrows pull together. "You're not to blame for it. I'm the one who decided to drink them." She pauses for a moment, falling serious, even though her eyes are glossy. "You know, he doesn't mean to be so hard on you. He just worries about you and really cares about you. You're his little sister and I think sometimes he feels like he didn't do what he could to protect you."

I stare at her and my breath catches in my throat. I know the words aren't coming directly from Sterling, but hearing them come from Olivia means the same exact thing. She wouldn't be saying these things to me if he hadn't confided in her.

"He did protect me. He's the best brother that I could have ever asked for. It's just hard trying to live up to someone like him."

"You don't have to live up to him, Stella," Olivia tells me, lifting her glass to her mouth as she drains the tiniest bit of liquid that's left in it. "You're your own person and I love the hell out of you. There's no competition between the two of you because you're both on your own journeys."

"I know," I admit quietly, not fully trusting my voice as Olivia brings out emotions I've been trying to ignore. "That's what I'm trying to figure out. My path and what my destination consists of."

Olivia stares at me thoughtfully from where she's sitting across the table. "Don't worry about the destination. That's in the future, and you'll know you've reached it once you get there. Focus on the journey and the present. And don't forget to enjoy yourself along the way."

"I'm trying," I tell her, the desperation evident in my voice. It's been a lot of work, trying to change the way I've been living my life and rediscovering who I really am. "Sometimes, I just can't help but let it get me down. Especially when I have my brother in my face questioning me like I'm not really putting in the work."

"Don't worry about him, Stella," Olivia tells me, slurring her words again as she attempts to flag down our server. "He doesn't know how to process things the proper way. You know how your brother is. He's a grump, but he means well, even if it may not seem like it in the moment."

"I know," I sigh, watching as our server walks over. Olivia holds up her glass, about to ask him for another mimosa, when I meet his eye and shake my head. "She doesn't need another, so maybe a water for her?"

Olivia pouts. "Are you really going to ruin my fun right now?"

"Yep," I smile back at her. "Water for you. Remember, we have your car, so Sterling's going to be wondering why I'm driving and not you."

"Shit," she mutters, and the word sounds half foreign coming from her. Olivia has never been one to really curse, except when she's feeling loose like this. "You're right. Water's probably best right now. What were we talking about, though?"

"You were lecturing me on my journey," I laugh lightly as I grab my own glass of water that I've been drinking since I finished my first mimosa.

"Yes!" Olivia exclaims, clapping her hands as she's brought back to whatever thoughts she had drifting around in her mind before she got sidetracked by wanting another mimosa. "Just enjoy the ride, girl. Let it take you wherever it decides to."

"You're right," I agree with her, smiling as she leans back in her seat. Olivia is more relaxed than I've seen her in a long time and I love seeing her like this. Not only is it the alcohol, but I know it has to do with my brother and how happy he makes her.

Hard to believe that an asshole like him could make someone this damn happy.

"You know... you and Simon," Olivia starts, a smirk creeping onto her face. "You two have some serious chemistry, and I've seen the way he looks at you."

A groan slips from my lips, my head falling backward as I close my eyes. "Don't even go there, Liv."

"Come on, Stella, don't be a prude now," she tells me, her voice playful. "I mean, I didn't ask any questions about what the two of you were doing in his room last night."

I lift my head, my eyes meeting hers. "And we're not talking about that."

"Just hear me out, okay?" Olivia pauses to thank the server as she takes her water from him and takes a sip. "Enjoy your journey and if he so happens to end up being a part of it, live it up, girl. I know you're not interested in relationships right now because you're trying to figure yourself out, but Simon doesn't want any of that either. If it happens, just roll with it."

"Why are the two of you sounding like you've been conspiring behind my back?"

Olivia lifts an eyebrow at me. "You know, maybe you should listen to the two of us. Tell me it doesn't sound like a good idea?"

I stare at her for a moment. Simon literally suggested the same thing, and I would be lying if I said it isn't tempting. Is it really the best decision I should be making right now, though? Things like that can always turn messy within the blink of an eye.

"I don't know, Liv," I tell her, my voice trailing off as I'm still momentarily caught in my own thoughts. "I mean, it sounds great, but there's always a chance of things going badly."

"Stop worrying about what could happen and just go with it, how about that?"

I stare at her with my eyebrows pinched together. "Who the hell are you and what did you do with my best friend?"

"You weren't the only one who had an awakening in life, girl."

I mull over Olivia's suggestion in my brain as it mixes with Simon's words from last night.

"You know what, fuck it. I'm just going to continue on my journey and whatever happens along the way happens, right?"

Olivia smiles back at me. "There's my girl."

I smile back at Olivia, not sure if I'm feeling as confident in this idea as she is, but she's right. It's time I start living in the moment again, but this time with a clearer head and no reservations.

I'm done making the same mistakes I have in the past, but I'm fully committed to enjoying this new journey I'm on.

And maybe I'll discover some new things about myself... with the help of Simon.

CHAPTER TWELVE
SIMON

Stella didn't get home until late last night. Lincoln and I were sitting on the couch playing video games when she came in. She didn't say much and I didn't want to push her after the conversation we had that morning. I still haven't figured out how I'm going to prove to her that I'm nothing like her brother.

Especially when I have to tell her I'm going to be leaving in a few days to head to Canada for hockey camp.

The next morning, Lincoln and I are sitting at the dining room table when Stella comes down. He's planning on staying around here for the summer and playing some of the different local leagues. The camp would be good for him too, but he decided he wanted to go a different route this summer.

"What are the two of you talking about?" Stella questions us as she takes a seat at the table.

Lincoln pushes an empty bowl and a spoon to her as she grabs the box of cereal from the table and the carton of milk. "We were just talking about when Simon is planning on leaving for Canada."

Stella's eyebrows tug together as she glances at me. She quickly recovers, her facial expression relaxing as she tilts her head to the side. "Canada, eh? What are you going there for?"

Fuck.

I wanted to talk to her about it, but I wasn't sure how to go about the conversation. We're not together or anything, so I'm free to go about my life as I please, but I didn't want to leave her hanging. Not with the possibility of having a fun summer fling with her.

"There's a month-long hockey camp I signed up for. It's something that will look good when I'm being scouted as a prospect."

Something passes over Stella's face and I can't quite put my finger on what it is exactly. Instead, a smile forms on her lips, but it almost looks forced.

"That's amazing," she says, her voice as sweet as molasses, but there's disappointment on the tip of her tongue. "I'm really happy for you."

"What are your plans this summer, Stella?" Lincoln questions her before shoveling a spoonful of cereal into his mouth.

Stella shrugs. "No plans, really. Just going to enjoy the break from California and trying to find myself in the process."

"Cool," Lincoln nods, and I feel like an outsider to their conversation, especially with the way Stella is currently avoiding my gaze. "I'll be around all summer since I'm playing in the local leagues. Looks like it will just be the two of us."

Oh fuck no.

There's no way in hell I'm going to let her spend the entire month with Lincoln fucking Reid.

The kid is like a brother to me, but I know how he is. Just because he was told Stella was off-limits, that doesn't mean he won't try and blur the lines. He thinks with his dick more than anything and if Stella lets him in the slightest bit, it's game over. He's charming and he knows it. And the last thing I need is for him to poach on my girl.

The logical part of my brain tells me he wouldn't

do that to me. He wouldn't do that to Sterling either. Lincoln isn't a threat and Stella already made it crystal clear she wants nothing to do with him. I shouldn't be worried about it at all, but I can't help but hate the thought of the two of them being alone here.

"Come to Canada with me," I blurt out, my gaze colliding with Stella's. Her eyes widen and I feel the same amount of panic running through me. Why the hell did I just suggest that?

I found an Airbnb that I was going to rent for the month while I'm there, but it's only a studio apartment in the city. Since I was just planning on it being me, I didn't plan for having a roommate, let alone having another bed for someone to sleep in. And here I am, offering Stella to come along with me.

Stella stares at me as a look of confusion passes through her expression. "And do what?"

Lincoln snorts out a laugh as he finishes his cereal and rises to his feet. "This is comical. Like, more entertaining than some of the shows I watch."

I give Lincoln the middle finger and he blows me a kiss before disappearing into the kitchen. Swallowing hard over the lump lodged in my throat, I look back to Stella. "I don't know. You could explore a new city and do whatever you literally want to do. Do you really feel like being stuck in Vermont for the entire summer?"

Stella falls silent for a moment. "No, not really."

"So, come with me to Canada. You can do whatever the hell you want to do while we're there. We can go check out the city and the things we've never seen."

"You're going to be busy with camp," she reminds me, tilting her head to the side with a look of amusement dancing in her eyes.

I shrug. "Only from, like, seven in the morning until four in the afternoon. I'm yours every evening, unless they end up having something planned during the camp."

My heart pounds in my chest. I don't know what the hell I'm actually doing here. I have no room for her to stay in and I don't know why the hell I just told her that I'm hers every evening. I mean, I'm not planning on going there and picking up girls, but my words could be taken a number of different ways.

Stella stares at me, still silent with a contemplative look on her face. The silence is killing me and I want some kind of an answer from her. It's a long shot. Why the hell would she want to go to a different country with me for a month? I can't help but want her to come along or else I would have never even mentioned it.

"You know what, fuck it," she says with a sigh before a smile tugs on the corners of her lips. "All in the spirit of rediscovery, right?"

I stare back at her as I let her words seep in. "You're absolutely right. What kind of journey would it be if it didn't include exploring new places?"

Stella smiles at me. "Count me in."

Fuck.

I'm excited and feel like my ego is soaring through the clouds right now. But there's just one problem. The living situation. And I'm not sure if I should tell her about it now or when we get there. I could always reach out and see if they have a two-bedroom instead, or something that would be a little better suited for two people to stay in.

"We leave in three days," I tell her, watching her as she rises from the table and collects her bowl. "Does that work for you?"

"I'm on your schedule, Simon. You tell me when and I'll make sure I'm ready to go."

I smile at her, caught in my head as I'm at war with myself. Stella turns away from me, heading toward the direction of the kitchen, when I find myself realizing I can't blindside her.

"Stella?"

She pauses in the doorway, turning back to face me. "Yeah?"

"So, I originally booked a studio apartment... so there's only one bed," I admit, my voice quiet as I suddenly feel nervous. My tongue darts out as I wet my lips. "I can call to see if there's a different unit available or something."

Stella nods. "I mean, whatever we have to do, we can make it work." She says the words with ease and shrugs as if it's nothing. "Surely there's a couch or we can get an air mattress if needed."

"So that means you're still down to go?"

A ghost of a smile plays on her lips. "Are you regretting inviting me along, Simon Murray?"

My eyebrows tug together and I shake my head. "Absolutely not."

Laughter spills from her lips and the corners of her eyes crinkle. "Good, because you're not allowed to take the offer back now."

She disappears from the room without another

word and I can't help but smile. This damn girl. I don't know what it is about her, but it's something intoxicating. I won't push her into crossing any lines because of the little personal journey she's on.

I'm just along for the ride...

Unless she decides she wants to ride me instead.

CHAPTER THIRTEEN
STELLA

We've already been in the car for hours. Simon made me get out of bed at the ass crack of dawn to make our trek to Canada. It's supposed to be a six-hour drive and it already feels like we've been in the car forever.

It hasn't been uncomfortable at all. I don't know if either of us are really morning people so we've both been fairly silent. We talked a little bit when we first got in the car and then I must have dozed off for the past hour. Lifting my head away from the window, I glance over at Simon who is humming along to the song that plays through the speakers of the car.

"Hey, sleepyhead," he says with a smile as he

glances in my direction and notices that I'm awake. "How was your little nap?"

"I don't know if I feel worse or not. I should have probably just stayed up the entire time." I glance out the window, taking in the scenery as we drive down the highway that is lined with trees. "Although, if someone wouldn't have made me get out of bed at the ass crack of dawn, I could have gotten a few more hours of sleep."

"I wanted to get there early to make sure we check in on time," he says, shrugging simply. "I have to check in at the rink and I wanted to make sure we are able to get into the room before I have to run there."

His explanation makes complete sense and I appreciate his consideration. I don't know what he has to do at the rink today, but I'd rather get situated in our room while he's handling the stuff he has to do. Simon was lucky enough to get us a different apartment that has two bedrooms. I don't know if he had to pull some strings or if the person ended up having an open one, but it looks like we'll be having our own beds, after all.

"How much longer until we're there?" I question him as I sit up straighter in my seat. Lifting my feet onto the leather seat, I cross them and prop my arms on my legs.

Simon glances at the GPS on the screen in his car. "We've only got forty-five minutes until we're there."

I didn't even realize that we were in Canada already until this moment. Since I was just waking up from a nap, it didn't register in my mind with how many hours we've been in the car that we would already be in a different country. Simon has my passport so he must have showed it to whoever when we reached the border.

The scenery around us doesn't look much different from Vermont. That's what it's like living in one of the New England states. We're surrounded by cities and wilderness. I'm not complaining because there's a part of me that does love it and missed it while I was in California.

Although, I'm really looking forward to exploring Canada. And I would be lying if I said I wasn't excited to do it with Simon. The two of us get along really well and I'm not going to even dive into the chemistry we have between us, because that has no place on a trip like this.

Simon is here for hockey and I'm literally just along for the ride. A place to stay while I explore something new in the world that I have yet to experience.

"You know, you snore really loudly," Simon chirps, breaking through my thoughts.

Whipping my head to the side, I cut my eyes at him as he continues to stare out at the road. "No, I don't."

"Babe, I just listened to you snoring the past few hours," Simon sighs, looking over at me with a knowing look. There's something playful dancing in his eyes and mischief plays on his lips. "Trust me. You snore."

"Do you have any proof?" I question him, feeling the heat creeping up my neck. Even though I've been with guys before, I've never had such intimate moments like I have with Simon. And me snoring isn't something I've had a guy ever tell me before.

I mentally kick myself. It's not like we're in bed or anything that it matters. I'm sitting upright in the car, so it must be because of the way I'm positioned. It's not like I snore often. I don't know what it is, but it's an embarrassing thought. I can see myself now with my mouth hanging wide open as I sound like an old man that has sleep apnea.

"Nope," Simon replies with his gaze still out the front window. "You think that I'm lying?"

Staring at the side of his face, my eyes are still narrowed on him. "I know that I don't snore loudly, so yes, I think you are. And considering the fact that you don't have any proof, it makes it hard to believe you're telling the truth. You have no evidence to support your claim."

Simon glances at me from the corner of his eye. "Okay, I over-exaggerated," he admits, a smirk pulling on the corner of his lips. "You do snore, but it wasn't very loud. Actually, it was kind of cute."

My heart pitter-patters inside my chest and my stomach does a flip. The embarrassment turns into something completely different. I suddenly feel shy and bashful, which is a foreign feeling for me. Simon has a way of making my emotions do a complete one-eighty out of nowhere. I swear, I can't even fully keep up with the range of things I feel when I'm around him.

Heat creeps up my neck, spreading across my cheeks, and I direct my gaze out the passenger's side window instead. I don't want him to see the pink tint on my cheeks right now. I don't want him to know the effect his words have on me, because I can't let them get to me like that.

We fall back into a comfortable silence and Simon turns the music up a little louder. He has no shame as he begins to sing along, and I honestly love the sound of his voice. It's some emotional song that I'm pretty sure I've heard in a *Grey's Anatomy* episode, but I can't remember the name of it.

His entire playlist while we've been driving has taken me by surprise. I didn't anticipate the wide range of genres and songs he's been playing, but I've honestly been vibing with it all. And who knew that Simon could sing like he does? Because I most certainly did not.

There's a hoarseness to his voice, yet there's something gentle and tender mixed with the sounds. I can feel it in my soul and I love the way the sound slides across my eardrums like the finest silk. Closing my eyes, I lean my head against the window and let the sound of his voice lull me back to sleep.

———

"Wake up, angel," Simon murmurs. I feel the weight of his palm against my shoulder as he gently gives me a shake. "We're here."

My eyelids flutter open and a warmth spreads through my body from his touch and the sound of his voice. Lifting my head, I look out the window and see that we're inside a parking garage. Turning to look at Simon, a small smile plays on my lips.

"Sorry if I was snoring again," I tell him sheepishly as I sit up straighter. The engine of the car is already turned off and I unbuckle my seat belt as I watch Simon push open his door.

"I was just fucking with you earlier, Stell," he chuckles as he winks. "You were saying my name in your sleep, though—that has my curiosity piqued."

My eyes widen and I swear I could die on the spot from embarrassment. I don't remember anything from my dream or if I dreamt at all, but either way, I'm completely mortified. "Oh my god..."

Simon laughs loudly as he climbs out of the car. He bends over, his gaze colliding with mine. "I'm kidding, angel," he smiles. "Chill out and let's go."

I cut my eyes at him but he closes the door before he catches the daggers that I'm shooting at him right now. This asshole. He's always so playful but I never know what to expect with him. I really believed him when he said that I was saying his name. Damn him for tricking me into thinking that I did.

As I get out of the car and push the door closed behind me, Simon is already waiting by the trunk with both of our suitcases. He doesn't bother grabbing any of his hockey equipment since he won't need it until tomorrow morning for the first day of his camp.

My eyes are still narrowed at him and Simon can't help himself with the smirk that's situated on his lips. His goddamn perfect lips... Shaking the thought from my mind, I follow after him as we head through the parking garage and to the apartment building. He stops out front, collecting keys from a lockbox that the landlord told him to use.

We find the apartment, which happens to be on the first floor, so it's not a far walk from the front door. I wait patiently behind Simon as he stops with both of our suitcases and slides in the key. He unlocks it, turning the knob as he pushes open the door.

His large hands are back on the handles of our suitcases, pushing them into the apartment with him. He stops short as soon as he's through the doorway and I collide into his back.

"What the hell?" I grumble at him, slightly irritated. It's like the feeling you get when you're wearing a pair of flip flops and someone steps on the back of them. You know it's an accident but you can't help but instantly feel annoyed.

"This isn't the apartment we were supposed to

have," he mumbles, not even paying any attention to me. "What the fuck."

Sidestepping Simon, I move around him and stop directly by his side as I see what he's seeing. It's not a two-bedroom apartment like he was told they were changing his reservation to. It's a goddamn studio apartment with one bed.

"I'm calling the landlord because this is bullshit."

Simon abandons the suitcases and turns around as he strides out into the hallway with his phone in his hand. I'm left standing alone in the apartment. I let my curiosity get the best of me and I meander around the space. It's a vast apartment for a studio. There's a full-sized kitchen, a living room area, and a bed tucked in its own little nook area. There's a full bathroom with marble tile and everything.

It's actually a really nice apartment, with every-thing modernized. I'm not saying I want to stay in this space with him, where there is literally no privacy, but I don't hate the room either. Walking to the kitchen, I run my hand along the marble coun-tertop just as I hear Simon walk back in.

His lips are tight in a flat line as he pushes the door shut behind him. A sigh slips from his lips as his eyes meet mine. "Looks like there wasn't another apartment available, so this is home for the next month."

I swallow roughly, offering him a small smile from where I'm standing across the room from him. The tension is already thick in the air, it's as if I can reach out and touch it. We had talked about an air mattress, but neither of us got one since we were under the impression that we would have two separate beds.

With Simon being the way he is, I already know he's going to make me take the bed while he takes the couch. And I appreciate the gesture, but that isn't fair to him. I'm the one who's practically imposing on his trip now—at least, that's how it feels.

"It's okay," I assure him, my smile bright on my face as I push away the anxious feeling that swims in my system. "We can make it work. It's not a big deal at all."

The air between us sizzles with energy and tension. We're going to be here for an entire month... sharing a studio apartment with only one bed.

What could possibly go wrong?

Everything...

CHAPTER FOURTEEN
SIMON

After leaving Stella to get situated in our new apartment, I head out to the rink. It's only about a fifteen-minute drive from where we're staying, but I have no idea where the hell I'm going. Thank God for GPS or I'd be completely lost in Canada right now. The traffic is atrocious on the way to the rink, so my fifteen-minute drive turns into a twenty-five-minute one instead.

I'll have to remember that for when I have to come here early tomorrow morning.

There are a few cars in the parking lot when I pull up, so I leave my stuff in the car since we aren't supposed to be doing anything on the ice today. It's literally just like a meet and greet and get signed in kind of thing. I've done numerous camps over the years of playing hockey, but this is the first time I'm doing a month-long one that is out of the country.

Walking through the front doors of the building, I can already feel the chill in the air as it slides over my bare arms. I'm used to the feeling, but it always brings me a sense of peace. Like on the ice is where I belong. It almost seems like it's something that should be humanly impossible, yet it's something we do every day.

Inhaling deeply, I smell the familiar scent of the rink. It's hard to describe it, but if you know then you know. There's a coldness that seeps into your system and you can feel it in your bones as it settles in your marrow. For some of us, hockey isn't just a sport. It's literally a part of us and something we could never ignore.

I walk over to the registration desk where two older women are seated. There are a few other guys here that are filling out some paperwork, but no one seems to notice me at first. I head toward one of the women and she lifts her head when she sees me approach, a huge grin on her face.

"Hi!" She smiles brightly. "Are you here for registration?"

"I am," I tell her, feeling a sense of pride as I give

her my full name to look it up in their system. It wasn't an expensive camp, but there are many people who try to get into it each year. In Canada, there are definitely more opportunities like this than there are in the States. But it still doesn't take away from how highly competitive it is.

Even though there were probably hundreds of applicants that were able to pay the fees to attend the camp, they pulled a curated list based on skill level. The rink offers other camps too, so that people of different levels still get the chance to attend. But for this particular one, it's literally the best of the best.

"Here's your paperwork, Simon." The receptionist smiles at me, handing me a clipboard with a small stack of papers. "It's just a few more waivers to go through and sign, as well as any health information, and emergency contacts." She pauses and her eyes meet mine with a knowing look. "I'm sure this isn't your first rodeo, so you know the drill."

"Yep," I smile back at her, taking the clipboard before I pick up a pen from the table. "I'll bring this back over when I'm finished."

"Perfect."

This is how it usually goes, whether it's for a league, a team, or a camp. You practically sign your life away when you sign up for a sport like this. Hockey isn't for the faint of heart. A lot of people don't realize how dangerous it can actually be and how fatal injuries can happen within the blink of an eye.

It wasn't talked about a lot, but considering the fact that we were skating on literal weapons, anything was possible. It didn't take much for a blade to cut through someone's skin and nick an artery. Or you had situations like Vaughn's. A bad play that ends your entire career. A blown knee that practically destroys your entire leg.

When you play a contact sport, you have to accept the potential consequences that might come with it.

When I was in junior high, there was a kid on another team that got hit with a puck straight to the chest. Even though he had pads on, it hit him directly in the heart and caused him to go into cardiac arrest. They weren't able to save him.

It's fucking sad and heartbreaking, but it's true. That kind of shit happens more often than the general public realizes. Not to mention the number of spinal cord injuries and players getting sliced from the blades of skates. It's a fucking tough-ass sport, so when you sign up to play, these places need to make sure that their asses are covered in case of a bad injury... or death.

After filling everything out, I take it back to the woman sitting at the table. She politely takes it and files everything where it belongs. She hands me a schedule for the week and gives me the rundown of how the camp works and what to expect throughout the days.

It's going to be long and fucking grueling, but this is what I signed up for and I'm fucking ready for it. After taking everything from the woman, I begin my own personal tour around the rink. She said I was free to look around and check out the locker room where we'll be meeting first thing in the morning.

The locker room isn't much different from your standard one, so I don't spend much time in there. Instead, I find the tunnel that leads out to the rink and I begin the walk down to it, feeling the coldness intensifying the closer I get. I reach the door and push down the button that unlocks it before pulling it open.

Staring out across the ice, it glistens under the lights that hang above. It's freshly cut and untouched. I love when the ice looks like this. Like there's something so serene and magical. It's also my favorite to skate on, which I think is the same for every player. You don't have to worry about any other marks in it from blades. You effortlessly glide across it like you're almost walking on water.

After staring at the ice for a few moments, I close the door and head back out. Stella is back at the apartment waiting for me and I want to take her out tonight as a way to thank her. I didn't fully expect her to come along and be so flexible with everything happening.

She knows how demanding my schedule is going to be, yet she doesn't seem to mind. Perhaps it's because she's looking forward to some time to herself as well. I couldn't help but feel bad about her being left in Wyncote while everyone else was leaving to go do whatever they had planned.

Stella is like a free spirit, yet I can't help but feel like she's partially lost. You know that saying, "not all those who wander are lost"?

I don't feel like that applies to Stella at all. She's as lost as they come right now, and I want to be the one who helps her find her way.

Even if it means she ends up going in the opposite direction of me.

When I get back to the apartment, it's quiet inside. I softly close the door behind me, my eyes scanning the area looking for Stella. Panic sears through my system and my heart pounds uncontrollably in my chest. My feet carry me through the apartment, and that's when I notice her in the bed.

Her dark hair pokes out from under the covers and it's a stark contrast to the white pillow her head is laying on. I didn't notice her at first with the way she's curled up in the center. She slept on and off on the car ride here, so I'm surprised to see her sleeping, but it was a long ride and I feel the same exhaustion.

We were supposed to go get dinner and explore the city tonight, but I can't help but be completely mesmerized by how angelic she looks right now. So peaceful and so innocent. The last thing I want to do is disturb her.

I finally pull myself away from the bed and wander out through the sliding glass door of the apartment that leads to our small patio space. Dropping down onto one of the chairs, I pull out my phone and find a local Chinese spot to order delivery from. After placing an order, I realize we have absolutely nothing as far as food or drinks in the entire apartment.

I'm not sure what Stella likes, so we're going to have to make a trip to the store. But that can wait until tomorrow. Tonight, I just want her to relax or do whatever it is that she wants.

Pushing out of my seat, I quickly check the time before heading out again. I run to a nearby convenience store and grab a six-pack of beer and a case of water. It isn't much, but it should get us through the night at least...

CHAPTER FIFTEEN
STELLA

Rolling over in bed, I realize that I fell asleep. *Shit.* I quickly sit up in a rush, throwing the covers away from my body. I only meant to lay down for a few minutes, but I must have been more exhausted from the trip here than I thought.

I jump out of bed in a haste, my bare feet hitting the hardwood floors before I start moving through the apartment. It doesn't register in my mind that I'm not alone until I'm in the living room area, noticing the TV is on and there's Chinese food spread out on the coffee table.

The door to the bathroom opens and I glance over, my eyes wide as I see Simon step out with a look of curiosity on his face. He tilts his head to the side, raising an eyebrow at me. "Where's the fire?"

A sigh escapes me and I shake my head as I try to fight the smile that pulls on the corners of my lips. "I woke up in a panic because I didn't realize that I even fell asleep."

A soft chuckle comes from Simon as he walks deeper into the room before dropping down onto one side of the sectional couch. "You're good, Stella," he says softly, patting the couch cushion beside him. "Now, come sit and eat with me before the food gets cold."

"Chinese?" I question him as I follow his command and sit down next to him.

Simon shrugs. "Who doesn't like Chinese food? We have nothing here to eat and I wasn't going to wake you up to go out. We can do that another night."

I smile over at him before reaching forward for a pair of chopsticks. Simon rises to his feet and I watch him as he walks over to the fridge. He comes back over with a six-pack of beer and I can't help but roll my eyes at him. "I see you made sure to get the staples."

Simon's face instantly falls and he freezes in place. "Fuck. I'm an asshole and an idiot."

My eyebrows pull together as I look up at him. "What are you talking about?"

"You don't drink. And I brought home beer."

"Simon," I start, my voice soft and gentle. He stares down at me and I'm momentarily lost in his steel gray irises. "Just because I'm not drinking doesn't mean that you can't drink either."

Simon sighs as he drops back down onto the couch. "I know, but I should have thought about it. I feel like a complete asshole right now."

I stare at him as I watch the torment wash over his face. "Give me one," I tell him, reaching out for one of the bottles.

"What? No," he argues, shaking his head at me. "I'm going to just take them back."

Frustration grows inside me. "Just give me a damn beer, Simon. Let me prove to you that I don't have a problem... that I can drink one and that be it."

"It's not that I don't believe you," he retorts, his voice strained. "I just don't want to be a bad influence on you."

I swallow roughly and keep my hand outstretched as I purse my lips. "Give me a beer. I'm not arguing with you anymore."

A wave of conflict passes through his eyes and

he runs a frustrated hand through his hair. "Fuck. Fine. But only one."

"Yes, daddy," I mock, rolling my eyes at him with a smirk. As soon as the words fall from my lips, I instantly regret them. A fire ignites in Simon's eyes and his jaw clenches as he stares at me. "I was just kidding. I don't know why I said that."

Simon stays silent for a moment before he hands me one of the cartons of food. "Just stop and eat, Stella."

There's thick tension that settles in the air and it feels like you could cut it with a knife. Part of me wants to argue with him because I don't usually just bow down, but with the way he's looking at me right now, I can't help but obey him. Twisting off the lid of my beer, I take a large gulp before setting it down on the table.

Simon directs his attention away from me and picks up his own carton of food before he digs in. Whatever is on the TV is quiet and literally just background noise at this point. I haven't once looked at it and even if I did, I'm pretty sure my brain wouldn't be able to focus on it.

His eyes are no longer on mine and I watch the way he dips his chopsticks into the noodles before lifting them to his lips. I'm mesmerized by the action, knowing exactly what his mouth feels like on the most sensitive parts of my body. Swallowing roughly over the lump that is now in my throat, I clench my thighs together before diving into my own food.

I don't know how the hell I'm supposed to focus on eating in these conditions, but I have no choice. Simon and I are just friends. He invited me along just so I could get away. I wouldn't have minded staying with Lincoln, but there was no way I was going to pass up this opportunity. Now that it's just the two of us in this small space, there's definitely a shift.

And it scares the shit out of me.

Simon's eyes find mine as he swallows a mouthful of food before washing it down with some of his beer. "Did you have any plans for tomorrow? I have to be at the rink by seven and I won't be back until later in the afternoon."

I shrug, attempting to act dismissive like him. Like there wasn't a sudden shift in the air between us. He can act like he's unaffected, so I'll do the same. Two can play this game and I'm fairly certain that both of us are sore sports.

"Nope. I figured I might go for a walk and see where the day takes me."

Simon raises an eyebrow. "Living life without any inhibitions?"

"I didn't say that," I tell him, adjusting in my seat as I set my food back down on the coffee table. "I just don't want to be locked into any plans. You know how they can often change. I'm here with literally no agenda. I'm just going to let life take me wherever it wants to."

He tilts his head to the side, a ghost of a smile playing on his lips. "I like it," he says, his voice soft and gentle. "Instead of controlling your journey, you're letting it become you. How freeing does it feel?"

His eyes are burning through mine and I feel like I'm being drawn deeper into the inferno. My skin feels hot, and my cheeks are definitely bright red right now. Yet, I can't pull my gaze away from his. "I don't know," I admit, my voice barely audible. "I'll let you know tomorrow, after my journey begins."

"You're already on your journey, angel," Simon tells me, and I'm lost in his steel gray eyes. "You just haven't let yourself fully experience it yet."

I don't know what the hell he's doing to me, but this wasn't part of the plan. Ignoring my beer on the table, I turn on the couch to face him fully. Simon's actions mimic mine and he's scooting closer to me, closing the distance between us. His palm is soft as he slides it across my cheek. His fingertips brush against my skin, slowly inching their way into my locks of hair.

His gaze collides with mine. "If you don't want me to kiss you, now would be the time to let me know."

My lips part slightly and my breath catches in my throat. "And what if I do want you to?"

I'm falling into the flames, completely consumed by his fire. His eyes bounce back and forth between mine briefly before his mouth crashes into mine. There's nothing gentle about the way his lips feel, yet they're so soft against my own. His kiss is brutal, and he bruises my flesh as he takes what he wants with nothing holding him back.

And in this moment, I will gladly give him every goddamn piece of me.

CHAPTER SIXTEEN
SIMON

I know I shouldn't be kissing her right now, but I couldn't help myself. I haven't been able to get her out of my mind for such a long fucking time. And now having her in such close proximity, I'm clearly losing any self-control that I possessed. After finding her in bed when I got back earlier, that's literally all I want.

I want her in my goddamn bed. Morning and night. Whenever the hell she will agree to being in there.

When we got here earlier today, I planned on sleeping on the couch and giving her the bed. Now I realize that there's no way in hell I'm going to be able to resist her. Unless she doesn't want me in the bed, we won't be sleeping separately.

Making a move on the first night is probably a bad idea. We still have an entire month we're going to be here, sharing this space. Anything can happen in that time frame. But you know what... Stella is on her own little journey, and maybe so am I. I'm on my own journey of doing whatever the fuck I want without worrying about what happens after.

What could possibly go wrong?

Our mouths are melting together. Stella parts her lips, granting me the access I crave as my tongue slides against hers. She moans into my mouth and I swallow the sound. Removing my hand from her hair, both of my hands are finding her waist and I'm pulling her onto my lap. Stella doesn't resist and she slides both thighs on either side of mine as she straddles me.

My cock is already harder than a fucking rock and it presses against her center through my pants as she settles on top of me. Her hands are on my shoulders and I can feel her warmth through the thin layer of my t-shirt. I'm ready to strip us both down to our bare bones and expose myself to her.

"I don't know what the hell you're doing to me, angel," I breathe against her lips as we break apart. Her breathing is shallow, her chest rising and falling in rapid succession. "Whatever it is, please don't fucking stop."

Stella shifts her hips, grinding herself on my cock through my pants. "We shouldn't be doing this," she murmurs breathlessly. "I can't get involved with anyone, Simon."

"Who said it has to be anything more than this, angel?" I question her, my fingertips digging into her flesh as I hold her in my lap. "You're just here for the summer. We can just go our separate ways, if that's what you want."

"So, we're on the same page then?" she asks me, shifting her weight again. Her palms are warm against my shoulders as she holds on to me.

Pulling back slightly, I lean deeper into the couch as I stare into her dark eyes. "I'm on whatever page you want me to be on."

Her eyes bounce back and forth between mine briefly. "Take me to bed."

My cock twitches against her and I waste no time. Sliding my hands to her ass, I lift her in the air as I rise to my feet. She's petite and feels light in my arms as I carry her through the apartment. When we stand side by side, she's more than a foot shorter than my six-three frame. She fits perfectly in my arms and it's effortless as I take her to bed.

This is not how I thought our first night here would go, but I don't think I would want this any other way. Stella's taking me along on her journey and I'm more than happy to oblige. I slowly lower her down onto the bed and drop to my knees as I pull her ass to the edge.

My hands find the waistband of her pants and I slide them, along with her panties, down her thighs until I'm pulling them away from her feet. Our gazes collide and Stella's eyes are wide as I push her legs apart with my arms. My face dips down to the apex of her thighs and I'm about to dive in when she slides her hands through my hair and lifts my head.

There's a touch of concern in her eyes. "What are you doing?"

"Finishing what we started the other night." I smirk, feeling the tug against my scalp as I fight against her grip and bring my mouth down to her pussy.

She tastes just like I remember and I run my tongue along her center. Her fingers are still tangled in my hair and she tightens her grip as I move to her clit. My tongue brushes over the most sensitive part of her body and her hips involuntarily buck, pushing her pussy against my face.

Lifting my gaze, I watch her as she's lying back

but propped up on her arms. Her head falls backward and her lips part slightly. I run my tongue along her again, circling around her clit as her chest rises and falls rapidly. A moan escapes her and I can't fight the grin that pulls on my lips as I know her sounds are from what I'm doing.

Her fucking moans are all mine.

I'm obsessed with the way she tastes and the way it's driving her mad. I continue to lap at her pussy, licking and sucking, tasting and teasing, until she's practically coming undone under my touch. Sliding one hand along the inside of her thigh, I don't stop until I'm sliding a finger inside her tight pussy. She moans loudly as I suck her clit in between my lips and begin to pump my finger in and out of her.

I've been with quite a few girls, but nothing equates to whatever this is with Stella. We both agreed that it's nothing more than a summer fling—just a simple hookup—and then we go our separate ways. But fuck... being between someone's legs while you fuck them with your mouth is on a completely different level of intimacy.

Sliding another finger inside her, I fuck her harder with my hand while rolling her clit under my tongue. I apply more pressure and she's coming apart at the goddamn seams. She's a breathless mess of moans. Her thighs are firm against my forearms, fighting against me as I continue to pleasure her in the best way possible.

"Oh my god, Simon," she moans loudly, her grip tightening on my hair. "I'm so close. Don't stop."

Disobeying her, I pull back slightly, but my mouth is still brushing against her pussy lips. "Come for me, angel," I murmur as I continue to pump my fingers in and out of her. "Come all over my tongue."

Stella pushes my head back between her legs and I dive back in, consuming her like a starved man. It doesn't take long before I'm curling my fingers inside her, pressing against the fleshy part that pushes her over the edge. Applying more pressure, I roll my tongue once more around her clit, and she's crying out my name, shattering into a million fucking pieces.

Her pussy tightens around my fingers and her legs are shaking as her orgasm tears through her body. Releasing her clit, I lap at her pussy, tasting her arousal on my tongue. My cock throbs in my pants, but I don't even need to be inside her right now. This is fucking enough for me.

My first taste of heaven.

Pulling my fingers from her pussy, I lift my head and move my arms away from her legs. As I move from my knees, a smile pulls on my lips when I see her. Stella is laid out completely on her back, her hair splayed across the bed. Her chest is rising and falling faster than I've ever seen it. She's completely breathless and I want to breathe life back into her.

The mattress dips under my weight as I climb onto the bed, crawling over her. I don't stop until my face is hovering above hers. Stella's eyelids flutter open and they are glazed over from the pure state of ecstasy she's in as she continues to ride out her orgasm.

"Jesus Christ, Simon," she murmurs, her voice barely audible. She lifts her hands to my chin, wiping away the wetness from when she came. "Whatever you were doing with your tongue should be illegal."

Tilting my head to the side, I raise an eyebrow as my face dips down to hers.

"If it were, I would gladly go to jail for making you come like that."

CHAPTER SEVENTEEN
STELLA

I've never experienced an orgasm like the one Simon just brought me to. It was like a goddamn earthquake, yet at the same time intoxicating and addicting. I wouldn't have a problem if he spent a majority of the time we spend together between my legs.

His mouth is back on mine and I can taste myself on his tongue. Lowering his hips to mine, he settles between my legs and I know I'm making his pants damp with how soaked I am right now. I can feel how hard his cock is as he presses it against me and I want to feel his entire length inside me right now.

Sliding my hands down to the waistband of his pants, I begin to push them down over his ass.

Simon breaks apart from me, his eyes searching mine as he hovers above me.

"Is that what you want, angel?"

I stare back at him, drawing my bottom lip in between my teeth. Simon's gaze drops down to my mouth before he captures my lip with his own teeth. He pulls it free from the grip I had on it and draws my flesh into his mouth. He bites down, leaving half-moon indents in my flesh, and it sends a shock wave through my body, the warmth spreading like wildfire.

He releases my bottom lip and runs his tongue over the wounds he inflicted before his gaze meets mine again. "That's my lip to bite, not yours."

I tilt my head to the side. "Oh, is it now? You think that you get to go down on me and now you're staking your claim on me?"

A chuckle vibrates through his chest and I swear to God I can feel the vibration in my pussy. "Here's how this little arrangement is going to work, angel. You're mine for the next three months and no one else's. If I see another guy even breathe in your direction, it will be his last breath. And I'm going to remind you every night when I get home whose pussy this is."

"You think it's yours?" I quip. There's a shift

from the playful side of Simon that I'm used to, but I would be lying if I said this isn't a huge turn-on. He might joke around and be lighthearted, but he's definitely an alpha when it comes to the bedroom. "Last time I checked, it belonged to me."

A smirk plays on his lips. "We'll see if you still feel that way after I'm done with you."

My breath catches in my throat and Simon moves away from me until he's standing at the edge of the bed. I lift myself up, sitting upright as he begins to pull his shirt up over his head. I can't help myself as my eyes travel across the curves and planes of his torso. His athletic form isn't surprising, but I wasn't expecting him to be chiseled like a damn sculpture.

"You too," he orders, motioning to my shirt with his hand. "Take it off."

The defiant part of me wants to challenge him and refuse, but I'm caught in the flames that are burning brightly in his steel gray eyes. I couldn't fight this even if I wanted to. Grabbing the bottom hem of my shirt, I lift it over my head before pulling my arms out. Simon grabs it from me and throws it onto the floor.

I'm almost completely naked, yet I still have my bra on. Simon slides his hands down to the waistband of his pants. They're pushed down from when I started to move them and I can see the perfectly cut V shape that disappears beneath his pants. He starts to push them down farther before he pauses.

He nods his head at me. "Let me see all of you, angel."

Swallowing roughly, I slide my hands behind my back and unhook my bra. The straps begin to fall down my shoulders, moving down my arms as I slide my bra away from my body. The air feels cold against my skin and my nipples instantly pebble from that and his gaze scanning my chest.

"You're a goddamn gift from the heavens."

His words have my heart crawling into my throat and I have no choice but to swallow it back. I can't let my mind go that way. We have an arrangement. Just a fling and nothing more. If he keeps saying things like that, I'm going to have to run away before I get too caught up in him. I'll have to leave before it's too late.

Simon drops his pants, his boxer briefs following along after them until they are both pooling around his feet on the floor. My gaze drops down to his cock and my lips part as a shallow breath escapes me. His cock stands to attention and with how hard it is, he's definitely ready to go. I can see a small bead of precum at the tip.

Scooting back on the bed, I watch as he steps out of his pants. A sinister smirk plays on his lips and he stalks toward me with a hooded gaze. He's the predator and I'm the prey. The way he's looking at me right now with the fire burning in his eyes makes it seem like he's going to devour me.

And there's not a single part of me that would dare to object to that.

Simon's hands find my thighs and he pushes them flat against the mattress as he settles between my legs. The tip of his cock presses against my center and I lift my hips to meet him. He stares down at me and I count three beats of my heart in my chest.

"I need to grab a condom," he murmurs as he nips at my lips with his own, planting his hands on the bed beside my head. "I'm clean, but I don't think the world is ready for any mini Simons running around."

I laugh softly at his words, watching the way his smile touches his eyes. "I'm on birth control, Simon," I tell him, my voice quiet. "We don't need to use a condom."

He pulls back slightly, his eyes searching mine. "Are you sure?"

I nod. "Positive," I respond as I pull my bottom lip between my teeth.

Simon claims my mouth with his own, drawing my lip between his teeth instead. "What did I tell you about this goddamn lip, angel?" He breathes against me as he runs his tongue over the half-moon marks he leaves in my flesh. "Mine."

Dropping down onto his forearms, he slides one hand under the back of my head as the other makes its way down to my ass. Gripping my flesh within his hand, he slowly presses into me. A gasp escapes me and Simon hisses as he slides deep inside me. He doesn't stop until he fills me completely, stretching me out like I've never been stretched before.

My body adjusts, taking all of him in, and I've never felt this full in my life. I've only been with a few guys before Simon and when it comes to size, literally not a single one compares to him.

"You good, angel?" he murmurs, his lips brushing against mine.

I smile up at him as he slowly begins to move his hips, fucking me gently. "Never been better."

Simon claims my mouth with his once more. He steals the air from my lungs, distracting me with his tongue as he lifts my ass higher to give him a better angle to fuck me deeper. I'm lost in complete oblivion as he kisses me with no inhibitions and continues to thrust in and out of me.

He's skilled and knows exactly what he's doing right now. The confidence radiates from him and its addicting. Hell, the things he's doing to my body right now are even more addicting. His lips are soft as he trails them along my jawline before moving to my neck.

My eyelids flutter shut and a moan escapes me as he gently sucks on my flesh, licking and tasting his way down to my collarbone. Abruptly, he pulls away and moves my legs from around his back. I stare up at him in confusion as he pulls out of me and climbs off the bed.

"What are you doing?" I question him, lifting my head as he bends over and wraps his arms around my thighs. A gasp slips from my lips as he quickly pulls me toward him, to the edge of the bed.

Flattening my legs against his torso, he holds on to my thighs and lifts me into the air as he slides back into me. This angle is so much more and I swear I can feel him in my goddamn rib cage. Warmth spreads through the pit of my stomach and

I moan his name as he slowly begins to fuck me again.

"Hook your ankles around the back of my neck, Stella," he growls, his fingers digging into my flesh. I follow his command and it lifts my hips higher into the air, giving him even more access inside. He slides in deeper and deeper with every thrust.

"Such a good fucking girl," he murmurs, sliding one hand down to the apex of my thighs. His thumb brushes across my clit as he holds both of my legs with his other arm. "You were made for this cock, angel. You take it so fucking well."

His words set my nerve endings on fire and he thrusts his hips, pounding harder into me as he continues to work his fingers across my clit. My hands grip the bedsheets as he pushes me closer to the edge. We're climbing to the top and it's suddenly a race to ecstasy.

Simon doesn't stop, he doesn't slow down. His eyes don't leave me as he fucks me into oblivion. My orgasm hits me with absolutely no warning, completely consuming my body and every thought. My face screws up, a loud moan escaping me as I shatter around him.

"Fuck, angel. I love this pussy." He thrusts into me. "So." *Thrust.* "Fucking." *Thrust.* "Much."

I'm a fucking mess, my legs shaking, my body quaking as my pussy clenches around him. I ride out the waves of my orgasm as Simon fucks me until he's about to come. He quickly pulls out, dropping my ass onto the bed as he roughly spreads my legs.

My body tingles and I feel the warmth of his release as he covers my pussy with it. I lift my head and I'm unable to look away as he coats me with his cum. When my eyes meet his, he stares at me in a daze with a smirk tugging on the corner of his lips.

"You are something fucking else, Stella," he murmurs as he lowers himself down onto the bed beside me, neither of us worrying about the mess we just made.

He wraps his arms around me, pulling me flush against his naked body. I don't fight him. Instead, I embrace his warmth and let myself revel in the way he feels and the way he makes me feel. I know this is all temporary but none of that matters at the moment.

Right now, Simon Murray is the only fucking thing that matters.

CHAPTER EIGHTEEN
SIMON

When I wake up in the morning, Stella is snoring softly, her head nestled in the pillow she fell asleep on. I'm still naked when I climb out of bed and I'm instantly missing her warmth as I stare down at her sleeping form. She looks so peaceful and I just want to slide inside her mind and see what she's dreaming of.

It's early in the morning and she doesn't have any solid plans for the day. The last thing I want to do is disturb her before I leave. She deserves to sleep, especially considering the fact that we didn't do much of it while we were in bed together. We gave each other quite the workout and I feel exhausted.

Thinking about going for a full day of hockey camp already has my body screaming in protest. I slip into some fresh clothes, not bothering to shower before I go. There's no sense, since I'm just going to get sweaty all over again. Plus, I can still smell the faint scent of her perfume on my skin and I want to fucking savor that smell for as long as I can.

I'm practically in a daze as I drive to the arena. After stopping to get a coffee and a pastry, it does nothing to help wake me up. I'm beginning to wonder if they gave me decaf by accident when I'm pulling into the parking lot. I find a spot and kill the engine before climbing out.

All of my stuff is already in the trunk, so I pull out my bag of equipment and grab my stick before closing the door. I made sure to slide a few Gatorades into my bag before we left Vermont. Probably not the best choice since they've been baking in my car from the hot summer sun, but oh well. When you're skating your ass off and needing a drink, it doesn't fucking matter.

They had already said that they would have food here and were going to feed us lunch and shit. So, I didn't really need to worry about it, but I brought them just in case. You never know what you're walking into until you're actually there. And I'm not usually one for being overly prepared, but something made me feel compelled to do so before my first day.

I'm greeted by some of the other guys as I reach the locker room. I recognize a few players who are also from the States. We played them on whatever teams they played for through their college. I don't have any problems with anyone I've ever played against, so it seems like everyone's going to get along fairly well.

The program director enters the room and tells us all that we need to meet on the ice in fifteen minutes. So time is limited to get our stretches in after putting on all our gear, but that's what we're here for. The on-ice and off-ice practice will both come in handy. Not to mention the various skills we will learn and work on perfecting.

It's all a part of the game and I'm in this for the long haul.

———

By the end of the day, I'm completely exhausted. Actually, that word doesn't even come close to how I'm feeling right now. I feel like I could collapse, pass out, and sleep for a week. It's been a long time since I've had a day like the one I just had. I knew these camps were intense—because I've attended them before—but holy shit.

This was only the first day. I can't even begin to imagine how I'm going to feel after five consecutive days of this shit. Not to mention having an entire month of it, except for the weekends.

When I get back to the apartment, I unlock the door and slide inside, but I find it completely empty. I got a text from Stella while I was in the middle of skating that said she was going out to explore, but that was from around noon. I texted her back when I was leaving to tell her I was on my way home, but she never said anything.

And now the panic is consuming me again. I walk over to the bed, half expecting her to be napping again, but defeat floods me as I pull back the covers and see she isn't there. Pulling out my phone, I quickly unlock it before tapping on her name to make a call. It begins to ring in my ear, and I hear it as it begins to vibrate from somewhere inside of the apartment.

What the hell?

She left and didn't take her phone with her. She went to go walk around in an unfamiliar city with no goddamn plans. And now she isn't here. How the hell am I going to find her? I don't even know where to begin to look.

I run a hand through my dirty hair. I had the opportunity to shower at the rink, but wanted to get back to her. Even though I smell like that lovely hockey scent, I couldn't get her off my mind and just wanted to see her. And I had every intention of showering as soon as I got home. But there's no way in hell that even matters now. Not with Stella missing.

Spinning on my heel, I begin to move toward the front door of our apartment, when I see movement outside of the sliding glass doors—the ones that lead to our own private patio. There shouldn't be anyone out there.

It doesn't help with my anxiety and I'm suddenly on high alert. The panic is even worse than it was when I realized that Stella isn't here. Now the thoughts of something absolutely horrible happening floods my mind and I'm suddenly marching directly to the door to find out just who the fuck is here.

My grip is tight on the handle as I slide open the door in a rush. It slams against the doorjamb and bounces back slightly as I step outside. Stella is facing away from me and she jumps, a gasp escaping her as she spins around to face me.

"Oh my god," she breathes, her eyes wide. "You scared the shit out of me."

Relief fills me, but it mixes with a little bit of irritation. "You're the one who scared me. I didn't think you were even here and was about to start a city-wide search for you."

She shrugs, batting her eyelashes at me with an innocent look on her face. "I'm sorry to worry you. I forgot my phone inside and wanted to come out here to relax until you were home." She pauses for a moment, her nose scrunching up in disgust. "Oh my god, Simon. You stink."

"You're so sweet, you know that?" I tell her, winking as I brush off her comment. She isn't wrong.

"And you're foul," she quips, laughing lightly. "Go get a shower and let's get food somewhere. I'm starving."

"Shit, we still need to go to the grocery store too."

Stella smiles at me sweetly. "Already done. Although, I just guessed what you might eat, so I'm sorry in advance."

I stare back at her and I can't even begin to

describe the emotions that flood me all at once. "You didn't have to do that," I tell her, my voice soft. "I was planning on going."

She shrugs dismissively again, as if it's nothing. "You were busy and I was out walking around. It seemed like a good time to do it."

"How was your walk, anyways?" I question her.

Stella shakes her head at me and waves me away. "Nope. I'll tell you all about it after you wash that stink away."

"Come get in with me."

Stella laughs. "Nice try, Simon. If you want to take a shower with me later, then consider it a deal. But right now, you need to wash that damn body before it comes anywhere close to me."

I love her attitude and the way she doesn't take my shit. I leave her out on the patio where she finds a seat at the table out there as I head back into the apartment. She made it clear she wasn't getting into the shower with me now, but she did say she would later... and I'm fully looking forward to that.

But first, I'm taking her out and treating her like the damn queen she is.

CHAPTER NINETEEN
STELLA

We managed to get through the first week of being in Canada without a hitch. Simon's been attending camp every day since that's why he came here. And I feel terrible every night he comes home. He's completely exhausted and worn down. You can see it in his eyes that his body just wants to crash, yet he refuses to let it happen.

Instead, he insists on keeping me busy and taking me out every night. We've gone out to dinner twice and explored the city the other nights after he let me cook for him at our apartment. Okay, he didn't actually let me cook, but I knew what time he would be home so I made sure there was food made by the time he got back.

Who would have known that my journey would have me acting like a housewife?

Part of me wishes this wasn't just a little fantasy world we were living in. Even when we go back to Vermont, things are going to change. There's going to be that weird shift where it's like none of this would have ever happened. I know we both agreed to this being a summer fling, but I don't know if it's going to even last that long.

It's one thing to almost be living a completely different life by being away from everything we know. We're in a different place, it's just the two of us, and no one else knows us or any of the people in our lives. When we go back to Vermont, it's like we'll be going back to reality. And then it will only be about a month and a half until I'll be flying back to the opposite coast.

The only thing I can do is enjoy this time we're having together, knowing this isn't forever. I'm just shocked... I never thought I'd be doing the things I have been for someone I'm not working to build a future with.

Come to think of it, I don't know that there is anyone I will ever end up building one with. Simon may be a fling, but he's setting the bar high. And this new version of Stella refuses to settle for anything less than she deserves.

This journey of self-discovery has been refreshing and I'm thoroughly enjoying it. I don't have to worry about the judgment from anyone outside of my own soul because it doesn't really matter in the grand scheme of things. No one else lives in my mind except for me. So, the only one who needs to be happy with who I am, is me.

I'm on the path to self-love and it feels... strange. It's different, but I like it. And I can tell Simon is enjoying it too. Especially with the way he's been burying himself in me every night.

We both slept in this morning as it's Simon's first day off since we got here. It's a Saturday and neither of us made any plans. We talked about it last night and decided we were just going to let the day decide where it was going to take us. I woke up before him and I can't disturb him. Not with the way he looks right now.

His dark eyelashes rest against his tan skin. I love the way his hair looks, when it's an unruly, tousled mess from rolling around together last night, and it's just another reminder of the memories that are now cemented in my brain. Regardless of what happens between us, I will never ever forget the moments we shared together.

My phone begins to vibrate from the nightstand and I quickly grab it to make the sound stop so it doesn't disturb Simon. I see that it's Olivia and a smile touches my lips. We've texted a few times since we both went our separate ways, but this is the first time we'll be talking on the phone.

I'm careful not to wake Simon as I crawl out of bed. Still naked from the night before, I find one of his t-shirts on the floor and pull it on before slipping out onto the back patio. I missed Olivia's call while I was getting dressed, so I call her back as soon as I quietly shut the door behind me.

"Hey, Stella," Olivia says, her voice cheery and bright. She's always been like the sunshine. I don't know how she manages to do it with my grumpy-ass brother, but they weirdly complement each other. Even if he is a dick to me sometimes. I know he treats her right and that's all that really matters at the end of the day.

"Hey, Liv," I smile as I say her name. "How are you? How is everything going?"

"I'm good! Everything's been going really well. We're settled into our new place. Sterling has been driving two hours back and forth to this damn camp that he signed up for."

"Why didn't you guys just go stay there?" I ask her, careful as I sit down on the chair for my ass to not show from under the bottom hem of Simon's shirt. I don't have anything on but that.

Olivia is quiet for a beat. "He said he didn't want to leave me and that we just got this brand-new apartment so it would be stupid to not stay here." She pauses again and I can hear the hesitation in her words. "I didn't really question him on it, but then it all made sense last night..."

My eyebrows pull together and I'm confused by her words. "What happened last night?"

"You know how we always talked about how much better life would have been if we were sisters?" she questions me, and I swear I can practically see the smile on her lips. "Well, it's happening. We're officially going to be sisters! Sterling proposed!"

Excitement fills me and I'm so elated for my best friend. I knew Sterling had plans of doing it eventually, but that was so fast. But then again, I guess the heart knows what it wants and when you meet that person who speaks to your soul, you just know.

"Oh my god!" I practically squeal. "I'm so

excited for you! Congratulations, girl! I don't know what the hell you see in my brother, but I don't even care. We're finally going to be sisters!"

"Yes!" she says loudly as she breaks out into a fit of laughter. "He completely caught me off guard, but it made sense why he wanted to stay here. He had it all planned with how he proposed at our favorite restaurant here. I wasn't expecting it at all."

"Come on, Liv," I shake my head, even though she can't see it. "You really didn't think he would propose? He's obsessed with you. I think you're the only person on the planet that can get him to actually smile."

Olivia giggles. "I mean, I hoped he would. But sometimes I still have to pinch myself to know that this is real life. He was always just a dream until he became more. It just doesn't feel real sometimes."

"I'm seriously so excited for you," I tell her with nothing but honesty. It's the best news I've heard lately. "What about the draft? Sterling should find out next month where he's going."

"Actually, he caught wind that he might be going to New York..." Olivia's voice trails off for a moment. I expect sadness because she's still working on her degree at Wyncote, but her next sentence completely surprises me. "I'm going to look into transferring somewhere, that way I can go wherever he goes."

My eyebrows pull together, even though she can't see the concern on my face. "Is that a smart decision?"

Olivia falls silent for a beat. "I would follow him to the ends of the earth, Stella. When you meet the right guy one day, you'll know exactly what I mean."

Turning my head, I glance inside the glass doors to where Simon is still sleeping in bed. Thoughts of him dance in my mind and I'm ready to go crawl back under the covers with him.

"I hope you're right."

CHAPTER TWENTY
SIMON

As I roll over in bed, I notice that I'm alone, but it's still warm where Stella was lying. I slowly sit up, stretching my arms above my head as I look around the studio apartment. She's nowhere to be found, yet again. As much as I'm happy for her and the way she's exploring life, I hate this feeling of her being a completely free spirit. It's like she doesn't think or care about anything that's really going on. She just drifts through the wind like a feather floating through the air.

There was a point where I thought she was lost, but maybe I was wrong. Perhaps she isn't lost, but she just doesn't want to be tied down to anything.

She's enjoying her journey and I can't fault her for that. That was the whole point of it, right?

I just hope that maybe when she does find herself, she'll find herself with me.

My eyes trail over to the sliding glass doors where I notice the curtains are pulled open. Squinting my eyes, I can make out her form sitting at the table. I rise from the bed, finding the bathroom to brush my teeth and relieve my bladder before I make my way toward the back patio.

Stella has a huge grin on her face and she says something into her phone before I watch her end the call she was on. My hand finds the handle and I slide open the door before stepping out onto the patio. Stella glances over at me, the smile still on her lips. My throat bobs as I see that she's wearing nothing but my t-shirt.

If she didn't already have a hold on me before, seeing her like this has me questioning everything in life.

"Can you just wear my shirts for the rest of forever?" I muse, my lips pulling upward as I take the seat opposite of her at the table. "It's a look that really suits you."

I watch the pink tint spread across her cheeks and her gaze breaks away from mine. She stares out at the trees that are lined around the back of the apartment building before she looks back to me.

"That was Olivia who called. Sterling proposed to her."

There's something off with the way she says it. Her voice sounds elated, like she's happy, but her face says otherwise. I'm not surprised Sterling didn't tell me. He had told me about a month ago that his intentions were to do so eventually, but he didn't give me any more than that. There's been a weird disconnect between the two of us and I haven't even really talked to him since he blew up on Stella.

Tilting my head to the side, my eyebrows pull together. "Are you not happy about it?"

"No, I am," she quickly recovers as her face lights up. "If there are two people who most definitely belong together, it's the two of them. I could not be happier for them."

There's still a vacancy in her words, even though I know she is being honest. "So, what's wrong, Stella?"

She's silent for a second, looking back out at the trees as she pulls her bottom lip between her teeth and bites down. I warned her what would happen if she did that, but I'm not going to intervene. There's something troubling her right now and that's more concerning to me than anything. She's somewhere else and not mentally with me right now. But just when I think I've lost her, she turns her head to look at me again.

"What if I never find happiness like that? I know there's more to life than love, but everyone wants it, right? What happens if I end up being one of those people who is alone forever?"

I stare at her, my breath catching in my throat. Her words catch me off guard. Stella has led me to believe she didn't want any attachments with anyone, yet she's contradicting herself right now. She might want to find herself, but somewhere along the way, she wants to find love too.

"You can't think like that, angel," I tell her, my voice soft and tender. "You will find love and you'll be at a place mentally where you won't accept anything less than you deserve."

"How does someone really know what they deserve, though? I just don't have a lot of hope. I've had nothing but failed relationships in the past because I was always trying to please everyone else."

I lean forward, resting my arms on the table. "Fuck everyone else, Stella. You do what makes you happy and one day your soul will find the one that complements it."

She's silent as she stares at me, but she nods as a pained look washes over her irises. I can't quite put my finger on the mix of emotions that swirl around in her eyes before she looks out to the trees again. She's working her way under my skin and I can't get her out of my fucking head.

I don't know what to do about any of this. We had an initial agreement that this would be nothing more than a summer fling, so why do I find myself not wanting summer to ever end?

———

Stella doesn't bring up anything else about her future or falling in love for the rest of the weekend. We have a pretty low-key one. I tried to get her to go out and explore, but she claimed she just wanted to stay in and watch movies. There's been a weird shift, almost like there's a distance that is growing between us.

I'm not quite sure what is going on or if I've done something wrong, but I've decided to just let it go for now. Part of me was actually thrilled that she just wanted to lay low this weekend. My body took a fucking beating from the first week of camp and I needed that time to recoup. Although, I'm not sure I can fully recover from all of the intense workouts until we're back in Vermont.

When we went to bed Saturday and Sunday night, neither of us made a move on each other, which was a stark contrast from the past week that I've spent buried inside of her. I wasn't about to make a move because it feels like I'm suddenly losing Stella. It's like she's putting a guard up in place and she's freezing me out.

I don't know why she's trying to push me away, but I can't let it happen.

I can't let her get away, even if we are just going to be in a situationship.

She's been in her mind and I know it has to do with the fact that her best friend and her brother are getting married. She isn't bothered by them actually being engaged, but I think it's really weighing on her mind with her own life. Perhaps it wasn't something that Stella ever thought was part of her plans, but now she's rethinking it. She's afraid she isn't going to properly fall in love...

And if Stella is going to fall in love with anyone, I want it to be with me.

CHAPTER TWENTY-ONE
STELLA

Things have been weird between Simon and me. I haven't been wanting to fully admit it or address it with him, but I feel like there's been a divide between us. I've been feeling myself getting closer to him and I don't like it. It scares me more than anything and the last thing I want to do is start to develop feelings for someone who isn't going to be reciprocating them.

This summer fling is turning into more of a headache than anything. I imagined that this would be something carefree, something that I wouldn't have to put much thought into. But now, things are getting more intense than that. He's the only thing that occupies my mind and I need to put some space between the two of us.

I can't let myself fall for someone who isn't going to be falling for me too.

Simon said all of those things about me finding love and it's what I really, truly want. When I'm in a place that I feel like I can give someone the same love in return. But I would be lying if I said I didn't wish it was him. There's something about him that draws me in and threatens to drown me in his ocean.

And when I really think about it, I find myself wading deeper into the water, feeling it brushing against the underside of my jaw. If I let myself get in too deep, I'll drown without a second thought.

And then what?

It would all be for nothing.

It's Wednesday evening. Simon has been seeming to be more and more exhausted every day and I've been using that to my advantage. We're in the middle of our second week in Canada and I can feel the time ticking faster. Everything is closing in on us and it won't be long before we'll be racing back to reality. And then all of this will be over.

I wanted to enjoy my time with him, yet here I am just pushing him away instead. It's a complete contradiction and it's all from self-preservation. I don't want to get hurt by getting my feelings involved, but I think that it's already too late. My feelings are very much involved and I already know that Simon is going to be the one to break my heart.

But maybe it isn't too late.

If I go back to California as soon as we return from Canada, then I cut our time short. Surely that would soften the blow to my heart? In fact, I might not even have it broken at all. I'm sure I'll still feel the pain and the hurt, but I won't suffer from the loss and I won't have a Simon-shaped hole in my chest.

He comes strolling into the apartment and I already have dinner made and laid out on the table for him. He's a little later coming home than he was last week, but that's because he started showering at the rink after camp instead. Speaking of which... we never did make it into the shower together.

I wince at the thought, instantly feeling guilty. I'm letting my own feelings get in the way of enjoying what's right in front of me. It's time for me to stop being so fucking stupid and just go with it and let whatever happen, happen.

"Hey, Stella," Simon says, his voice almost flat. It's been a few days since he's called me angel and I didn't realize how much I liked hearing that word come from his lips. "You know, you don't have to make dinner every day. I'm able to cook or can always grab something on my way home."

I stare at him for a moment, my eyebrows pulling together. His gaze doesn't meet mine as he walks into the kitchen to grab a bottle of water before taking a seat at the table. I know what he's trying to do here and I can't say I don't blame him. This has all been a mindfuck for the two of us and I'm not making things any better.

Swallowing roughly, I take a seat across from him, watching him carefully as he puts some of the salad on his plate before handing the bowl to me. "I'm sorry, Simon," I tell him, the words falling from my lips in a rush.

His steel gray eyes meet mine and he raises an eyebrow at me. "For what? You didn't do anything wrong."

"But, I did," I tell him, my voice sounding small. There's a part of me that wishes the ground would open up and swallow me whole. No one likes to admit when they're wrong and this is most definitely an uncomfortable conversation to be having. "I went and made things weird between us and I owe you an apology for that. I didn't come to Canada with you for things to be awkward between us."

Simon stares at me, his fork in his hand as he tilts his head to the side. "Are we having an honest conversation here? Or are we just going to tiptoe around the truth?"

This time it's me who's raising an eyebrow. "What truth would we be tiptoeing around?"

"The fact that you're trying to push me away. If you want to have a real talk about it, then tell me why."

Shit.

I can't tell him why. If I tell him why, then I'm laying everything out there for him to see. I'm revealing all of my cards, and I don't feel confident enough to do that. Judging by the curiosity on Simon's face, he really doesn't have a damned clue. And I'm not about to be the one who lets him in on the little secret I've been keeping.

And that secret is, I have goddamn feelings for him.

"I told you that I didn't want to get involved with anyone," I start, making sure I choose my words carefully. "I need to focus on myself and you've been blurring my thoughts. This won't go past this summer and I know when I'm starting to get attached to someone—whether it's as a friend or romantically."

Simon's metallic eyes burn holes through mine.

"And which is it this time? As a friend or romantically?"

Goddammit. Simon frowns as I hesitate, but I'm not even sure what to say. I can't be honest with him about my feelings, but I can't sit here and lie to him. Not when he has me backed into a corner with nowhere to run.

"Both."

His frown vanishes, but his jaw clenches as he nods. "So, what do you want to do about it, Stella?" he questions me, his voice low and calculated. "If you don't want to get attached and you want space, please tell me how we do that while living in this fucking studio apartment."

I can't tell if he is pissed off or hurt. He sits completely still in his seat. His tone isn't angry but he is not happy. That much, I can tell.

"I don't want the space."

"You're contradicting yourself, Stella," he informs me, as if I didn't already know. "What do you want?"

I swallow hard over the lump lodged in my throat. "You."

He's silent as he tilts his head to the side. "Then I'm yours for as long as you'll have me. But stop trying to push me away. I'm not going to play games with you, angel. If you decide you don't want me, that's fine, but I need you to be straight up with me. Can you at least do that for me?"

"I don't want to play games either," I admit, shifting uncomfortably in my seat. "I just can't let my heart get involved. Our lives are completely different. We live on two different coasts. There's no way anything could work after I go back to California."

"Stop thinking so far into the future," he says simply as if it's the easiest thing to do. "Just worry about what is happening in the present moment. Nothing is guaranteed except for this moment."

"How can you say that when you've been working your entire life to set yourself up for your future?"

Simon falls silent as he chews on my words. "That's a good question and one I honestly can't answer fully. I have hopes for the future and want it to be something I'm going to enjoy, but I can't guarantee that it's going to happen. I don't know, Stella. Maybe I'm not the person who should be giving you advice."

I tilt my head to the side, raising an eyebrow at him as I process his last sentence. "Why would you say that?"

"Because I'm involved with someone I have feelings for, even though I know it's going to end sooner rather than later." He pauses for a moment and I swear all of the air leaves my lungs in a rush. "So, I don't have any advice or answers for you. If I were that concerned with my future, don't you think I would be worrying about how the hell I'm going to recover after you tear my heart to shreds?"

Every single word completely leaves me. I stare back at him, my eyes wide as I struggle to breathe. Simon abruptly drops his fork onto the table before he pushes his chair back in a haste. There's frustration and pain swirling in his irises and I want to reach out and wash it away.

But he doesn't give me a chance.

Instead, he heads out onto the back patio, leaving me completely alone as his words hang heavily in the air. I've been so concerned with my own self-preservation, I didn't fully take his into consideration.

Simon has feelings for me, and there's only one thing left for me to do to make this right.

I have to be honest with him.

I have to let him into my heart.

CHAPTER TWENTY-TWO
SIMON

Standing out on the back patio, I lean against the railing as I stare out at the row of trees. Frustration runs rampant through my system and I can't seem to calm myself down. My heart is pounding in my chest, threatening to break through my rib cage. I shouldn't have walked away from Stella, but I royally fucked up this time.

We agreed to let this be a fling and I went ahead and just laid it all out for her. She was trying to push me away before I admitted everything to her and now I went and opened my damn mouth. She's probably inside packing her shit as I stand out here. I wouldn't be surprised if she already has her flight back to California booked.

I can't say I would blame her. She made it clear what her intentions were and I should have respected the space she was trying to put between the two of us. She didn't want her feelings to get any deeper and I just pushed everything over the goddamn edge now.

The door behind me slowly slides open, but I don't turn around to look at her. I don't know if I can face her right now. My feelings are something I usually keep close to my chest, and here I am just spilling them all out for her. I fucking admitted that I know she's going to break my heart.

What the hell is my goddamn problem?

"Simon," Stella approaches me, her footsteps light and her voice soft. "Can we please talk?"

Swallowing roughly, I slowly turn around to face her, letting out the breath that I was holding as I see her standing in front of me. She looks like she's been sent to me from fucking heaven and I don't know that I ever want to let her go. I shouldn't have all of these emotions and wants with her, but I can't help it. The heart wants what it wants.

"I'm sorry for telling you all of that," I admit, my voice hoarse and rough. "I should have just kept it to myself, but honestly, I couldn't any longer."

"It's okay," she says, her voice soft like silk. "I don't want you to ever apologize for being honest with me. I'm the one who needs to apologize, because I haven't been fully honest with you."

Her words hit me like a blow to the chest, but yet there's something that flutters in my stomach. A feeling that's similar to hope and it's one I don't like to explore. Hopes and dreams usually end up being crushed.

"What do you mean?" I question her, my voice quiet because I don't fully trust it in this moment.

"When I said I could feel myself getting attached, that was barely touching the surface of my feelings. We agreed on this just being a summer fling, but I don't know if I can honestly do that." She pauses as she wrings her hands in front of her. "I want more, Simon. And that's what scares me the most."

My heart skips a beat at her words and I can't help it as I take a step closer to her. "What do you want, angel? What do you mean by more?"

"I want it all. I want everything with you," she says softly as she takes a step toward me. Reaching out, I cup both sides of her face with my hands. "I don't want this to end after the summer."

"Neither do I," I admit, my face dipping down to hers. "If you're going to fall in love with someone, I want it to be me."

I hear the sharp intake of her breath but it's too late as my lips are crashing into hers. Stella steps closer to me, wrapping her arms around my back. Her lips part slightly as I run my tongue along the seam, letting me inside. Our tongues tangle together and there's nothing gentle about the kiss. It's filled with urgency and need.

I need her in more than just a sexual way and she finally knows.

I can only hope that this doesn't blow up in my face. Stella has her reservations about the future and she has every right to be. I just need her to get lost in the moment with me and we'll worry about what comes after later.

Removing my hands from her face, I drop them to her shoulders before sliding my palms down her arms. I wrap my fingers around her elbows, pulling her arms away from my waist. I don't know what the hell we're really doing. She admitted she feels the same way, but I know Stella better than she realizes. If she thinks she's going to get hurt, she's going to run in the opposite fucking direction.

But I can promise that I will always follow her.

———

We're back inside, both of us on the bed as we strip each other of our clothing. Our mouths only break apart as we remove our shirts. Stella's hands are on my body as mine explore every inch of her skin. Grabbing my shoulders, she attempts to roll me onto my back, but her strength is no match for my own.

A chuckle vibrates in my chest and I don't fight her as I give in and roll onto my back. "Take what you want from me, angel."

Stella stares down at me with a fire burning in her irises. My cock is throbbing as it lies against my stomach. She reaches down for it, pumping it twice before she folds her body in half. Her lips are soft and warm as she wraps them around the tip. I inhale sharply as I watch her head bob and she practically swallows my cock in one movement.

A moan escapes me as her mouth reaches where her hand is holding me by the base. Her mouth is wet and warm and I could lose myself in her in an instant. I'm feeling like a goddamn schoolboy, ready to bust a nut before we've even gotten around to having sex.

Stella bobs her head a few times, her tongue stroking my cock. Sliding my hand through her hair, I grab a handful and grip her hard as I control the movement of her head.

"Jesus fucking Christ," I murmur, feeling my balls already beginning to constrict as I lift my hips. "I love your lips around my cock, angel. Swallow it fucking whole until I'm coming down your throat."

She doesn't stop, as if my words are only encouraging her more. Her grip around my cock tightens and she continues to bob her head, taking my cock in and out of her mouth. As she lifts her head once more, her lips are still around the tip before I pull her head away from me.

I release my grip on her hair and she stares down at me with confusion in her eyes. Her plump lips are bright red and wet from sucking my dick. "I changed my mind."

Stella tilts her head to the side. "Did I do something wrong?"

"Fuck no," I growl, sitting up slightly as I grab her hips and pull her onto my lap. "I would rather come deep inside that sweet pussy instead of your mouth. And if you didn't stop now, it wouldn't be long before you'd be swallowing my cum."

A smile lingers on my lips as she lifts her hips and positions my cock. The tip presses against her center and a groan falls from my lips as she lowers herself, sinking down onto me. Stella moans at the same time, her hands landing on my chest as I grip her hips tightly.

"Fuck," I growl again as she rolls her hips before lifting them. "Ride that cock, angel. It was made for you."

"Whatever you want, Simon," she moans as she begins to bounce up and down on my cock. "Are you done with me yet?"

Her question throws me off and I stop her on my lap as my eyebrows pull together. "Absolutely not. Why would you even ask that?"

"Because you said that after you were done with me, we would see if I still felt the same way... that I don't belong to you."

I take the bait. Hook, line, and fucking sinker. A smirk pulls on my lips. "You change your mind already? You ready to admit that you're mine. That this pussy is mine," I say as I brush my thumb across her clit. "That this body is mine," I continue as I run my hands up her torso, stopping as I place my hand over her heart. "That this belongs to me."

Her lips part as a ragged breath escapes her. "I'm yours, Simon."

Sliding my hands up to her face, I grab her throat before jerking her down to me. "That's right, angel. And no one else's."

"No one else's," she repeats before she claims my lips with her own. With one hand around her throat, I move the other to her ass and grip her flesh as she begins to move on top of me again. She shifts her hips, fucking me harder.

Lifting both of us up, I roll her onto her back and settle in between her thighs. Stella wraps both of her legs around my waist and I hold on to her ass with one hand, lifting her hips higher into the air as I begin to pound into her. My other hand is still around her throat, but my grip isn't tight.

I fuck her harder, thrusting into her over and over again. Her pussy begins to tighten around my cock and she's a mess of moans as she comes apart at the seams. It doesn't take long as I continue to pound into her, stroking her insides with the length of my cock, before she's coming.

"Don't stop, Simon," she moans loudly as her orgasm tears through her body. It's like a goddamn earthquake. Her pussy is like a vise grip as it tightens around my cock and her legs begin to shake. "Oh my god!"

The sound of her voice, the way her face looks as she loses herself in the pleasure I bring her, is enough to send me falling over the edge. I pound into her once more, filling her to the fucking brim before I'm coming deep inside her. My balls constrict and draw closer to my body as the warmth erupts through my body.

We're both riding the high of each other and our orgasms. Removing my hand from her throat, I slowly fuck her until she's filled with every drop of my cum. I slowly pull out of her, resting on my knees between her legs as she lies there breath-lessly. Stella lifts her eyes to mine, her face flushed and her chest rising and falling with every breath she takes.

I look down at her pussy and can see my cum starting to leak out. Taking my finger, I run the tip through our arousal before pushing it back inside her. "That's all for you, angel. I want you to feel my cum leaking from your pussy all night long. I want you to think about me inside you while we're out."

Lifting myself off the bed, I go to grab my clothes and begin to pull them on. Stella rolls over onto her side, still breathless as she stares at me. "What are you doing?"

"Getting dressed," I tell her as I lay her clothing on the bed. "I'm taking you out tonight."

"Where are we going?" she questions me as she slowly sits up and puts on her bra.

My eyes meet hers once more as I wink. "You'll see when we get there."

CHAPTER TWENTY-THREE
STELLA

The city streets aren't very busy, but Simon stays close to me as we walk to a destination he still hasn't informed me of yet. I didn't ask him any more questions after we got dressed and headed out the front door. He said I would see when we got there, so I guess I'm in for a surprise—whatever it may be.

It's the middle of summer and the days are warm but once the sun sets, the air has a chill to it. I wrap my sweater tighter around my body. Simon slides his arm around my shoulders and pulls me against him, his warmth enveloping me.

"Are you cold?" he murmurs, his voice soft against my ear as we continue to walk.

I shake my head. "That little bit of breeze was just chilly, but I'm okay."

Simon stops walking, pulling me to a stop with him. He releases me as he pulls his sweatshirt over the top of his head and hands it to me. He's left in just a t-shirt and a pair of joggers. "Wear this."

I hold it in both hands, a black hoodie with the Wyncote Wolves emblem on the front in white. It's massive compared to my small form and I lift my eyes to Simon's. "This isn't going to fit me."

"Nope, but it should keep you warm."

"Aren't you going to be cold?" I question him as I take off my sweater and pull his hoodie over my head. The arms are far too long and the bottom hem stops at the middle of my thighs. The hood is up over my head and I leave it up to block out the cool breeze. My hair tickles my back underneath Simon's sweatshirt so I reach inside and pull it out, letting it fall down over my breasts.

Simon tilts his head to the side, a ghost of a smile playing on his lips. "Don't worry about me, angel," he says softly, his hands finding the sides of the hood. He adjusts it slightly, his steel gray eyes burning holes through mine. "I like the way this looks on you."

He takes a step toward me, but releases the sides

of the hood. His one hand falls down to mine and he threads our fingers together. "Come on," he says as he turns away and begins to walk back down the street. I follow along after him, his palm warm against mine.

I let Simon lead me through the city as I look around at the tall buildings and lights. It's a different slice of the world and I've been loving exploring every inch of it. Every city that I've been in has its own little personal touch and if I'm being honest, this one might be one of my top favorites.

We fall into a comfortable silence, both of us admiring the architecture of the buildings around us. Simon leads me down another street and it's a little busier than the others we were on. This one is lined with different stores and restaurants. For a moment, I think he's going to take me to one of the places to eat, but I don't have much of an appetite right now.

Instead, he pulls me across the street to a court-yard-looking area. He leads me to what appears to be a garden area with massive hedges but as he leads me past them, it's actually like some sort of a maze. It reminds me of *The Secret Garden* from when I was a kid.

"What is this place?" I question Simon as the

two of us walk hand in hand through the rows of hedges. There are different displays of flowers scattered throughout. It's truly something magical and it almost doesn't even feel like there's an entire city moving around outside of these green walls.

"I didn't even know this place was here until I looked it up on Google," he admits, a shy smile playing on his lips as he glances down at me. "It's one of the city's most popular attractions. They put in a bunch of the wildflowers to help with the bee population. It really adds a nice touch, like a small slice of nature that we so often forget about when we're in the industrial side of the world."

My eyebrows tug together. "I didn't know you cared so much about nature."

Simon shrugs. "Not as much as I should. I try to be cognizant of it all, though. We're all our own worst enemies, destroying the only planet we have actually inhabited."

"There's really a lot about you I don't know."

Simon stares at me and I watch as a smirk pulling on the corner of his lips. "Stick around and get to know me, angel."

He scares the hell out of me, but I find myself falling for him with every moment between us. If I sink into him any deeper, there will be no way for me to get out. Even if I attempt to claw my way to the surface, he will permanently be embedded in my soul. Simon's like a stain that you can't wash out and he's already left his mark on me.

We both fall silent, but Simon's hand doesn't leave mine as he begins to lead me back through the rest of the maze. I have no idea where we are going and after our second dead end, I'm fairly certain we have sufficiently gotten lost in this damn thing. I must say, it's been a pleasant experience, though.

And then it's as if the universe hears my thoughts and we step through the clearing, where we reach the center of the maze. There's a massive fountain in the middle and it's breathtaking. The water cascades down various crevices and flows into the pool that is around it. It's an abstract, marble piece of art, almost as if it's left for the consumer to interpret whatever it is.

"Wow," I breathe as he leads me up to it. There are a few people around it, marveling at its beauty, but none of them even matter. I'm entirely captivated by the piece of art in front of us that functions as the most magnificent fountain I've ever seen.

I turn to look at Simon and he isn't even looking

at the fountain. Instead, he's staring down at me with a storm brewing in the depths of his eyes. "Isn't it beautiful?" I ask him, my voice catching in my throat.

Simon's throat bobs as he swallows roughly. "The most beautiful thing I've ever seen."

Instead of staring at the fountain, now I can't tear my eyes away from his. He steps closer to me, closing the distance between us as he slides his hands into the front pocket of his hoodie that I'm still wearing. He tugs on it, pulling me closer to him before wrapping his arms around my back.

"I don't want this to end, Stella," Simon murmurs against my lips as he holds me tightly against him.

"No one said it has to," I tell him, pulling back slightly as I tilt my head. "We still have time together."

Simon shakes his head. "Summer is almost over, angel. I know we talked about going our separate ways afterward, but what if I don't want that? What if I told you I want more with you?"

His words steal the air from my lungs and my eyes widen as I stare back at him in shock. "You were never part of the plan," I whisper, not fully trusting my voice. I can't hold back the words and they simply escape me before I have the chance to swallow them back down.

Simon raises an eyebrow at me. "I didn't think you fully had a plan. I thought you were just figuring it out as you went along."

"Yeah, but I told myself I wouldn't get involved with anyone else, and here I am."

His throat bobs and his fingers dig into my skin as he pulls me even closer. It's almost as if he wants to pull me into his body until we become one entity together. "So, what now? I want more and you don't."

"I never said that," I retort, shaking my head at him. "I don't want this to end either, but it's not that simple, Simon."

"What if it was? No one said it has to be complicated."

"Everything is always complicated," I remind him, a small smile playing on my lips. "And there's always a price to pay."

Simon rakes his teeth over his bottom lip but he doesn't challenge me any further. I can see it in his metallic eyes that there's something running through his mind. There's more he wants to talk about and he isn't done with me yet, but he doesn't push the issue.

Instead, he captures my mouth with his own, silencing the thoughts of self-doubt and the questioning of our future. Simon distracts me in the only way he knows how and makes my body sing under the moonlight in the middle of the garden.

CHAPTER TWENTY-FOUR
SIMON

Stella and I didn't talk about what she said that night. We've fallen into this comfortable situation together. I'm not quite sure what else to call it. We're not in a relationship, but I'm not fucking around with anyone but her and I know she's on the same page.

It's like we're living in our own little fantasy, dream world. We only have a few weeks left here in Canada before we have to go back to Vermont. And that's when we will be forced to face reality.

But the reality is, I don't want this to end then. I want to go back home to Vermont and have Stella by my side. Whether she moves back or stays in California. I'll travel coast to coast for that fucking girl.

She doesn't realize just how serious I am right

now. I haven't pushed it too much because I don't want to scare her off before we leave Canada. I've made it clear what my intentions are and I know Stella isn't stupid. She knows what this is, even if she's terrified of it.

"All right, guys," our coach says as we wrap up our practice. "As you all know, we're going to have a draft at the end of the week. After that, you will only be working with your teams for the next two weeks before we begin the tournaments."

I glance around at the other guys as I take my helmet off. A few of the guys have become friends of mine, but it is just a summer thing and we are all here from all over the world. I'm sure I wouldn't see any of these guys again, unless we end up playing in the NHL together one day.

"What team do you want to get on?" Alex, one of the defensemen I had become friends with, says. He pulls his helmet off too as we stand on our skates on the ice. "I wonder if they're going to tell us who the top three picks are."

I shrug, knowing I'm not going to make the top three. There's a lot of really skilled players here and it's extremely competitive. I know better than to hurt my own feelings by assuming anything. "I doubt it. I know they're trying to make shit seem realistic, but I don't see how that would be beneficial to anyone."

"I guess we will find out on Friday," Alex says, tapping my head with his gloved hand. "You wanna go out tonight? Some of us are going to go hit up some bars and you haven't been out with us yet."

I stare at him for a beat, not sure how to respond. "I brought a friend along to stay with me while we're here and I feel bad leaving her at the apartment by herself."

Alex raises an eyebrow. "A girlfriend?"

A chuckle vibrates in my chest. "It's complicated, but that's the plan eventually."

"Bring her along," he says with simplicity, almost like I'm an idiot for assuming she couldn't come along. "If she doesn't care how some of the guys are."

I smile at him. "Stella has been around hockey players her entire life. She knows how we can all be."

Alex laughs as we head off the ice. "Perfect. Meet us at Jim's around seven."

After finishing up at the rink, I head back to the Airbnb Stella and I are staying at. When I walk inside the studio apartment, I can't seem to find her again. Instead, there's a note left on the kitchen counter in her cursive handwriting.

Went for a walk and stopping at the store while I'm out.
If you need anything, call me.
Love,
Stella

I know a lot of people put 'love' at the end of their notes out of habit but I can't help but smile at it as I reread her note again. My heart beats erratically in its cage and I don't bother trying to stop it. That's just the effect Stella Barrett has on me and there's no sense in fighting it anymore.

She might still be scared shitless of the idea of getting involved with someone, but I'm not. I'm ready to take the plunge and fall into the abyss of her love.

Pulling out my phone, I send her a text to let her know that I'm home and going to get a shower. I also add in about the guys inviting us to come out before I plug my phone into the charger. She doesn't respond at first, so I leave it as I grab my clothes and take them into the bathroom. I turn on the water and let it heat up as I check my phone once more.

STELLA

I'm on my way back now. That sounds like a plan for tonight!

A smile pulls on my lips and I slip out of my clothes, tossing them into the hamper before I type a response back to her.

SIMON

Hurry back and meet me in the shower.

Locking the screen on my phone, I set it back down on the dresser and walk away before waiting for a response from her. That way she will see that I never got her message. Maybe it will make her more inclined to join me.

As I slip into the shower, the water is scalding hot, but that doesn't stop me from stepping under the stream. Reaching forward, I turn the handle to make it a little colder and immerse myself in the heat as I let it soothe my tired muscles. That's one thing about this camp—it's no joke and works my body harder than it's ever been worked before.

After standing in the water for who knows how long, I finally grab my shampoo and begin to work a lather in my longer strands of hair. Through the foggy glass doors, I see Stella's silhouette as she walks into the bathroom. She's silent, turning to face me as she begins to strip out of her clothes, leaving them on the floor by her feet before she steps closer to the shower.

My breath catches in my throat and I step back into the water, rinsing out the shampoo as she pulls open the door and slips inside. I'm completely mesmerized and lost in her as she steps into my space and shuts the door behind her. Her hands find my chest, moving like silk through the water as she pushes them up to my shoulders.

"There's my girl," I say softly as I push my hair from my face and find her hips with my hands. Pulling her naked body flush against mine, I spin us around, putting her under the stream of hot water. "I missed you today."

Stella tilts her head back, her long dark hair hanging down to her ass as the water soaks it. I lift my hands from her hips and run my fingers through her hair. "You don't miss me every day?" she asks quietly, lifting her head to look at me.

"Every goddamn second that I'm not with you."

She cocks her head to the side, lifting an eyebrow. "Sounds like you've got quite the obsession."

"That doesn't come close to touching what I've

got for you," I murmur, spinning her around as I push her back against the shower wall. A gasp escapes her, but I capture her mouth with my own, swallowing the sound. My tongue slides along the seam of her lips and she parts them as she lets me in.

I kiss her until she's out of breath and then I'm releasing her as I slowly begin to make my way down her torso, kissing my way down her body. Stella's chest heaves with every shallow breath as I drop to my knees in front of her.

She doesn't protest as I lift one of her legs, hooking her thigh over my shoulder. I swear to God, this is my fucking favorite place to be. Sliding my hands along her thighs, I don't stop until I'm gripping her ass and sliding my tongue along her pussy.

Stella slips her hands through my hair, gripping the locks tightly as I fuck her with my mouth. She holds on to my head for dear life as I work my tongue against her, rolling it around her clit. Flattening my tongue, I apply more pressure as I move against her, driving her closer and closer to the edge.

She's a complete mess, her hips bucking against my face as she wiggles against the wall. Gripping her ass, I hold her in place as I continue to move my tongue against her.

"Jesus Christ, Simon," she moans as her body grows tense. My cock throbs between my legs and I want to dive so fucking deep into her pussy. "I'm so close. Don't stop."

And I don't.

I don't stop until she's shattering into a million pieces, screaming my name as her orgasm tears through her body. Running my tongue over her, I don't stop tasting her until she's done. Only then do I stop, but only long enough to stand up and spin her around.

Sliding my hand along her spine, I urge her forward. "Bend over for me, angel," I murmur, pressing my cock against her wet center. She doesn't fight back as she folds her body at the waist, dropping her hands down to the stone bench seat in the shower. "Good girl," I tell her as I slowly thrust into her.

Stella presses her ass back against me, a moan escaping her as I fill her to the brim with my cock, feeling my balls pressing against the apex of her thighs. I stop for a bit, savoring how it feels to be this goddamn deep inside her. It isn't the first time but I'm sure I'll never grow tired of it.

On my knees with my face in between her legs

might be my favorite place to be, but I could stay like this forever with my cock inside her.

"What are you waiting for?" Stella groans, pressing her ass even harder against me as she attempts to work her hips and fuck me herself.

My grip tightens on her hips and I hold her in place. "That's not how this works, angel. As hot as you look right now, pushing back on my cock, I'm the one who's going to be fucking you."

Pulling back until it's just the tip inside her, I pause for a few seconds, my eyes traveling across her naked back before I slam into her. Stella screams out in pleasure. I slide my hand in front of her, my fingers making their way to her clit as I continue to pound into her.

I fuck her until we're both coming apart at the seams, Stella shattering around me into a million pieces as I lose myself deep inside her. We're soaring through the sky on a cloud of ecstasy and I never want to come back down.

I want to stay like this inside her forever, just like she is inside my soul.

Stella has the most fragile part of me, and she has no idea.

CHAPTER TWENTY-FIVE
STELLA

Simon ate me out and fucked me in the shower before washing my body like the tender, loving person he is. I had only ever known his playful side before and I was enjoying getting to know this different side of him—Simon Murray as a lover instead of a friend.

The only problem is, he wants more—and I'm not sure I can give him that.

I know what will happen in the end. Not all of us are as lucky as Olivia and Sterling. We don't all get a happily ever after that is wrapped neatly with a pretty bow. Simon is graduating next year, while I'll still be in college. He'll be going to the NHL, and who knows what the hell I'll be doing.

I have an entire life I am building in California

and Simon has his in Vermont. Something like that would never actually work. Long distance isn't my thing. Hell, I couldn't even do short distance with Trey. After that failed relationship, I'm a little jaded.

Do I think that Simon is going to do me dirty and sleep around behind my back? Not necessarily. But at the same time I think I would be a fool to believe that no one would do something like that. When you're too busy falling in love with someone, it's easy to be blind to the bad shit that is happening around you.

"Stella, this is Alex and Liam," Simon says as he introduces me to two of the guys from the hockey camp. There's a huge group of them here, but Alex and Liam are the two who greet us when we arrive at some dive bar called Jim's.

"It's nice to meet you both," I tell them, smiling as I shake their hands. "Where are you both from?"

"I'm from Seattle," Alex tells me, winking. "Simon tells me you live on the West Coast. You know, California isn't that far from Washington."

Simon possessively wraps his arm around my lower back, pulling me flush against his side. "Fuck off, Alex," he growls at him, practically snarling. "She's mine."

"You said she's just a friend, though..."

For some reason, hearing him say that stings, but I swallow back the feeling and shake my head at the two of them, forcing out a laugh. "Both of you, calm down. Sorry, Alex, but Simon is right. I'm already spoken for."

I can feel him relax against me and he presses his lips to my temple. "Thank you," he murmurs against my skin.

Liam clears his throat. "I'm from Michigan," he offers, shrugging as everyone turns to look at him. "What? She asked and you all looked like you needed a diversion."

I smile at him, laughing quietly. "I like you. You're smart."

Liam winks at me. "Who wants shots?"

Simon's body goes rigid against mine and he abruptly turns to face me as his friends disappear toward the bar. "Fuck, Stella. I'm a goddamn idiot. I didn't even think about coming to a bar... I just wanted them to meet you and I forget sometimes about the drinking, you know?" He runs a frustrated hand through his hair and I can see the turmoil on his face. "We can leave."

"Simon, stop," I tell him as I cup the sides of his face. His eyes bounce back and forth between mine. "I am fine."

"Are you sure?" Simon's eyes continue to desperately search mine, his expression soft and gentle. "None of these guys matter. Only you do, and I don't want you to feel uncomfortable."

Lifting up on my tiptoes, I press my lips to his before pulling away. "I promise I'm fine. Let's get back to your friends?"

Simon's throat bobs as he swallows hard and nods. "Okay," he practically whispers. I pull my hands away from his face and he slides his fingers through mine before we head back over to the bar. There's one empty seat and Simon lifts me up into it before he moves behind me, wrapping his arms around me as he holds me close.

"Are you going to come to the tournament games?" Liam questions me as he hands me a water and Simon the beer he ordered.

I smile at him. "I wouldn't miss them."

Simon has managed to keep hockey separate from me while we've been here but I know he would want me to be there. The way he holds me a little tighter after I say that lets me know how much he does. It's a chance for me to see him in action and watch him do what he loves. There's no way in hell that I'm going to pass up that opportunity.

We spend the rest of the night with the guys and

they are exactly as I imagined. It's funny how predictable hockey teams are. There always seems to be the playboy who likes to test the limits, which would be Alex. The goofy one who is just kind of floating through life, in this case Liam. There's always a grumpy one, who is another player I was introduced to earlier named Victor. And there's the sweet, golden retriever—Simon.

There's always a few others that fit the same description or have similar qualities. These were the only ones who I remembered after meeting so many different guys from the camp. And Simon made it a point to make sure that each and every one knew I was completely off-limits.

It warmed my heart, the way he was protective and possessive, but it also clouded my thoughts. I was lost in my own head most of the night, even though no one seemed to notice. I could tell by the way Simon looked at me as he slowly sipped the single beer he ordered for the night—he knew what was going on.

He knew I was running through every scenario of how this could possibly work.

And I'm sure he knows that there's no way it ever will.

Our lives are just far too different. What am I

supposed to do? Up and leave college when he gets drafted into the NHL? Give up everything that I have been working for, for myself to be with him? I'm only now just figuring out who I am. I can't lose that to become an extension of Simon.

I need to be my own person.

And I'm going to have to break his heart in order to do that.

———

"A penny for your thoughts?" Simon questions me as we step through the door of our Airbnb. "I know you, Stella. I've watched the wheels turning in your mind all night, even with everything going on around us. What's going on?"

I swallow roughly as I keep my back to him and head over to the dresser that has my clothes. "I think I need to head back to California."

The air in the studio apartment grows thick with tension and Simon is completely silent, it's almost as if he isn't here. I pull a change of clothing out before I turn around to face him. He's standing in place like a statue with his eyes on me.

"Why?"

"I've run through literally every scenario in my

head and it just doesn't work. We're only kidding ourselves and remember, it was just supposed to last for the summer." I pause while trying to push through the emotion that is building inside me. "Summer is almost over."

Simon doesn't say a word, he just stares at me. I watch as a shadow passes over his expression and suddenly, he's headed directly toward me. My body is frozen and I can't get my brain to work quick enough to tell my feet that they need to move.

He enters my space, his hands cupping the sides of my face as he tilts my head back. He drains the oxygen from the room and I feel like I can't fucking breathe. Can't think. I need the space, but I don't want him to give it to me. Tears prick the corners of my eyes and I can't even fight against them as they begin to spill over.

"Tell me you don't feel this between us, angel," he breathes, his voice strained. "If you can look me in the eye and tell me I've been imagining this the entire fucking time, then I will let you go. I'll let you walk out of that goddamn door and my life and I won't try to stop you."

My lips part but he shakes his head as he brushes his finger across my mouth to let me know he isn't finished.

"But if you can't, I can't let you go, Stella. I will never give up on you and us being together. I'll follow you coast to coast, country to country, to the ends of the fucking universe. I don't give a fuck what it takes, but I will make you mine."

My breath is caught in my throat and my heart skips a beat as it tries to keep up with the demand of the emotions rushing through my system.

"Tell. Me."

I shake my head, pulling my gaze from his as I look past him. "I can't, Simon. I can't fucking tell you that because I do feel this. I feel all of it and it scares the shit out of me."

"Don't try to run away from me, angel," he says softly. "You'll never be able to outrun me."

"It will never work," I tell him, not giving up my stance on the issue. "You have your life and I have mine."

"What is there for you in California anymore? A douchebag ex-boyfriend and the friend who fucked him behind your back?" Simon shakes his head. "Leave it all behind and be with me."

My eyebrows tug together. "Do you hear what you're asking of me? You want me to give everything up and just live the life you're living."

"No, not at all. If you want to go back to California and stay there, fine. But I told you, I will follow you wherever you go."

"You're not giving up what you have in Vermont for me, Simon," I tell him with an edge in my voice. He's being irrational, unreasonable, and absolutely insane. "Don't be stupid about this."

"I'm not," he argues. "There are hockey rinks all over the world; there's only one of you."

I stare at him as my heart pounds against my ribcage. "Why are you making this so goddamn hard for me right now?"

A smile pulls on the corners of his lips.

"Because you're mine, Stella. And I'm never giving you up."

CHAPTER TWENTY-SIX
SIMON

I can see the turmoil in Stella's expression. She doesn't know what to do.

"Don't make a decision right now," I tell her as she looks up at me. "Just wait until after we get back to Vermont. This is all part of your journey, remember?"

Stella's lips pull downward into a frown. "I can't make a decision when I'm this close to you. You cloud my thoughts, you make me feel things that I've been avoiding feeling. I think I need space to process and figure out what I want to do."

Her words feel like a blow to the chest, but there's a part of me that has no choice but to be understanding. I may not fully agree with it even though it does make sense. She's too close to the situation she's trying to make a decision about.

"What do you need from me, angel?" I ask her, brushing the hair away from her face as I tuck it behind her ears. "What can I do to help?"

Stella stares back at me with an indistinguishable look in her eyes. "I need you to let me go."

What the fuck?

My jaw clenches, my eyes widening before I narrow them at her and shake my head. "No."

She reaches up, her hands wrapping around my wrists like she's going to move my hands away from her face, but instead she just holds on to me. "What do you mean no?"

"I can't and I won't do that."

"Why not? You asked what I needed from you and I told you." This time she pulls my hands away and takes a step back. "I need space to think, to clear my head, and to do that, I need you to let me go."

"I have no problem giving you space, but I'm not going to let you go, Stella."

She lets out an exasperated sigh. "You're absolutely impossible, you know that, right?"

I smile at her. "I never once implied that I was anything different."

"I'll stay until your hockey camp is over, but then I'm going back to California for a little while."

Her words catch me off guard and as badly as I want to beg her to just stay, I know I can't. She's asking me for space and I have to give it to her. Stella's been trying to figure out who she is and what she wants out of life. If I push her too hard, that's only going to push her away.

She's already jaded after what happened in her last relationship. There's a part of her that doesn't trust me simply on principle even though I've never given her a reason not to trust me. If she wants to go back to California to figure things out, I can't stop her.

"Whatever you need, Stella." I take a step back from her. "If you want space, then I will give you that. But just so we're clear... I won't wait forever for you to come back to me. If you take too long, I'll come for you."

She fidgets with her hands in front of her and I want to desperately pull them apart and distract her from the internal fight she's experiencing right now. As much as it kills me, I can't be physically close to her. She needs space and has made it clear that being close to one another only clouds her thoughts more.

Turning my back to Stella, I grab a change of clothes and head into the bathroom to get ready for bed and brush my teeth before I come back out. Stella is standing in the kitchen area, drinking a glass of water with her back pressed against the counter.

She watches me from where she's standing as I walk over to the bed and grab one of the pillows. I grab my charger for my phone and take both over to the couch. There's an outlet right by where my head will be, so I plug it in and set my alarm before grabbing a blanket and making myself a bed.

"What are you doing?" Stella asks me as she walks into the living room area.

I glance up at her as I lie down on the couch and cover myself up. "Going to sleep. I have to get up early for camp. We have our draft on Friday and I want to earn some extra points to hopefully get on one of the better teams if I can."

She's silent for a moment. "I meant, what are you doing on the couch?"

My emotions are all over the place but I can't let Stella know that. As badly as I want to influence her decision, that's not the type of person I am. I won't manipulate her thoughts. Instead, I shrug with indifference and direct my attention to the TV as I turn it on. "I'll be sleeping on the couch the rest of the time we're here."

"Why?" she questions me with zero hesitation.

"Because you said you want space, Stella. If you don't want space, then say that. I'm not going to play these back-and-forth games, though. I know what I want and what I want is you." I pause, my gaze meeting hers. "Until you figure out what you want, I'm putting some distance and space between us. I'm here whenever you decide."

She stares at me like I just broke her favorite toy from her childhood. It might hurt her right now, but it's the goddamn cold, hard truth. It's not fair to either of us, and what good will it do if I keep sleeping with her and fuck her every night when she doesn't know if I'm what she wants or not?

It's not going to do a fucking thing to help either of us.

So, instead, I'll wait for her.

And if she decides she doesn't want me, I'll pick up the pieces and move on.

By the time Friday rolls around, I'm honestly just ready to be done with this damn camp and go back to Vermont. I don't want Stella to go back to the other side of the country, but sharing an apartment with her is killing me right now.

I barely even pay attention during the draft. Much to my surprise, I get picked third and end up on the powerhouse team at the camp. Alex and Liam are both on the same team as me and they can barely contain their excitement as we head back to the locker room to collect our things.

"Are you okay, Murray?" Alex questions me as we step inside the room. Our lockers are side by side, so we walk over together. "You seem off or something."

I glance over at him as I grab my bag and stick. "I don't know. I just got some shit going on that has me a little distracted."

"You know you're gonna have to check that shit at the door," Liam reminds me as he walks over to us with his stuff. "From what I hear, Coach Cole is quite the hard-ass."

"Yeah, I know," I tell both of them, putting on a facade of being fine. "I'll be good when we start practice next week." The three of us fall silent as we follow the rest of the guys out of the room and exit the building.

"Trouble in paradise with your girl?" Alex asks when the three of us reach the parking lot.

"Something like that," I tell him with a shrug. "She doesn't know what she wants and wants some space."

"Ah, shit," Liam says, shaking his head in disappointment. "That's never a good sign."

"What do you mean?" I ask him.

"Wanting space pretty much says what she wants already. She's trying to let you down easily, and she's just trying to figure out the nicest way to do it."

"Or she's hoping that the space will make you move on to someone else," Alex adds.

The two of them are getting in my head and confusing me even more. As if it wasn't already bad enough that Stella wanted space... now I'm wondering if there's more to it like the guys pointed out. Maybe she really does know what she wants. And it isn't me.

"Come out with us," Liam says as we stop at his car. "Alex and I are going to go grab dinner somewhere now and then drink the night away."

I look between the two of them and weigh my

options. I can either go out with them and drink away the thoughts of Stella or go back to the apartment and spend the night in the awkwardness between us.

"Fuck it, I'm in," I tell them with a shrug. "Who's driving?"

CHAPTER TWENTY-SEVEN
STELLA

Lying in bed, I roll over again for probably the fiftieth time. Things between Simon and I have been strained and awkward, but today has been exceptionally different. I spent the evening alone, ate dinner alone, and was now going to bed alone. I had been going to bed alone all week, but Simon was here every night when I went to sleep.

Now I was lying in bed in an empty apartment in a strange city.

He texted me earlier, around the time he should have been back from hockey camp, and told me he was going to be going out with some of the guys and not to wait up for him. My heart sank the minute I read the message. There was such an indifference in his words. I know that tone can easily be misinterpreted through text, but it was so short and to the point.

I was the one who put this wedge between us but my fear made it seem valid. There were too many variables about the future. I know I came here to be on this journey of self-discovery with no plan. I don't know if I can continue that after this summer. Whatever this is between Simon and I can't continue when I go back to California.

Either we come together as one or we're going to need to go our separate ways.

Grabbing my phone from the nightstand, I check the time and see that it's already close to eleven o'clock at night. Simon's camp ended at four, but they had their draft today afterward. He texted me around five-thirty, which is when he told me he'd be back when he left this morning.

I scroll through my messages again to see if there is anything from Simon, but there isn't. I end up on Instagram, checking his account to see if he happened to add anything to his story. There's nothing. I check Snapchat. Nothing.

Simon was never really one to post often or

share anything in his stories, but I thought it was worth a shot. Just as I go to lock my screen and set my phone back on the nightstand, I hear the lock turning on the front door to our apartment.

There's a loud commotion and the door slams shut. Something clatters onto the ground, followed by the sound of keys hitting the floor.

"Fuck," Simon slurs from the door. I slowly sit up, flicking on the light as I see him bending over to pick up the stuff he dropped. He sways as he stands upright again and stumbles over his own feet as he reaches the counter before setting his things down.

He whips his head over to look at me, his eyes bloodshot and glossy. "You're still up."

"I am," I respond, my voice calm and collected even though I want to walk over to him and shake him. "Did you drive here?"

Simon shakes his head. "No, I left my car at the rink and rode to the bar with Liam. I think I got an Uber here. Or someone brought me here. I don't fucking know."

I've never seen him drunk and in this state before. It's strange and equally frustrating. He's not his happy self like he normally would be. Even though things have been tense between us, he had still been pleasant to be around up until this moment.

"Well, I'm glad you didn't drive," I tell him, not quite sure what else to say. "Why don't you get comfortable on the couch and I'll get you some water?"

Simon ignores me and makes his way to the fridge before he pulls out a beer. "I don't want any water."

I slowly begin to climb out of bed and my footsteps are light against the floor as I pad over to him. "Simon, you're already wasted. You need to sleep it off."

"And you need to back the fuck off," he sneers, slurring his words together as he twists off the cap to the beer and takes a swig. "What I do doesn't concern you anymore, Stella."

"Why would you say that?" I stare at him, hurt and confused. "Everything you do concerns me."

Simon sets his beer down and turns his body away from mine. "Just stop fucking lying already. Please, just save the bullshit. I know what you're doing."

His words are like a knife to my heart. "What are you talking about?"

"You don't want me. You're trying to buy yourself time to let me down easy." He turns his head back to look at me again. His eyes are wild and bloodshot. "Just do it already, angel. Break my heart now instead of prolonging the inevitable."

"None of that is true, Simon," I assure him, taking a chance as I make my way closer to him. "That's not true at all. I said I needed space because I need to think this through. You know the way our futures are going and I need things to align."

Simon lets out a harsh laugh as he grabs the beer and pushes off the counter. He stumbles in my direction, catching himself on the other side of the counter. "Things will never align, Stella. You either make it work or you don't. People make sacrifices and that's how shit works. Clearly, you don't want to be the one who has to make any."

It feels like he's twisting the knife, pushing it farther into my heart. "I never said I don't want to make any sacrifices. I just need to know that it's worth the risk in the end."

"Stella, do you hear yourself? You need to know that it's going to be worth it in the end? How the hell can anyone know that? No one can predict the future and if you live your life that way, then you're not really fucking living."

His words hurt. I know there's truth behind

them but I can't help but feel extremely upset by what he's saying to me. The thing is, I don't let myself display emotion in front of other people when I'm upset. Simon isn't going to see that he's hurting me with his words. Instead, I use anger as a buffer for my emotions. It's a nice cover-up for how I'm actually feeling.

So, that's what Simon is going to get.

He won't see that I'm upset. He's going to see that I'm pissed off and irate.

"What the fuck is wrong with you, Simon?"

He tilts his head to the side and leans against the counter with most of his weight. "Absolutely nothing." He smirks. "Most people don't like hearing the truth, so I'm sorry it hurts, angel. It hurts me too."

"Fuck you. It doesn't hurt you. You're wasted and completely out of pocket right now. You're talking out of your ass like you have an idea about what you're saying."

"You're wrong," he argues as he pushes himself upright. "I mean partially. I am wasted, but I know exactly what I'm talking about. I really have no right to be mad at you for it. I agreed to it from the start, but that was before I fell in love with you."

My breath catches in my throat as his six words linger in the air between us. Simon drains the rest of his beer and stumbles through the living room until he successfully lands on the couch. He's fully clothed and still has his shoes on as he rolls onto his back.

"I was never supposed to love you, I know," he continues with absolutely nothing holding him back. "That was my fuckup. If I could unlove you, I would. It never occurred to me that you wouldn't want to be with me. I thought I could make you love me back, but I was fucking wrong."

I'm literally frozen in place, my feet are cemented to the floor. I stare at Simon who isn't even looking at me. He's staring up at the ceiling, struggling to keep his eyes open from how drunk he is.

"You know, some girl approached me at the bar. I could have gone home with her tonight, but I didn't." He pauses as he kicks his shoes off. "I turned her down as soon as she came over because all I could fucking think about was you."

My heart crawls into my throat and I can't fight the tears as they spill from my eyes. The room is too dark, even with the bedside light on. Simon can't see my face, he can't see my emotions pouring out as they stream down my cheeks.

"I never once gave you a reason not to trust me,"

he says quietly, still slurring his words. "I know your ex cheated on you, but that doesn't mean I will. It's like you think I'm going to be just like him and that fucking hurts, angel. I'm not him and you never even gave me a chance to show you that I'm not."

"Simon..." I start, my voice cracking before trailing off.

He doesn't hear me.

"Maybe it is better if you just go back to California."

Everything stops. The world around me stops moving. Time is suspended and it feels like I'm suffocating. Somewhere after the words came out of his mouth, the oxygen dissipated from the room around us and I suddenly can't breathe.

But I don't make a move. I don't make a sound. I just stand there and stare at him in disbelief, feeling my heart as he rips it directly from my chest.

He's got all of this wrong. He's drunk and the things he's saying are things he wouldn't normally say if he were sober, but that's where the issue lies. There's a saying that a drunken mind speaks a sober heart.

He admitted that he's in love with me, only to turn around and tell me I should leave in the next breath. It's like whiplash, which I'm sure is what it had felt like I was giving him by saying that I wanted space, when in reality, I don't know what I really want or wanted.

"Is that what you want?" I ask him, my words a far whisper as I don't fully trust my voice. Everything feels and sounds foreign. It's like this is a bad dream and I just want to wake up from it.

Simon yawns and rubs his eyes. "It would make the most sense, don't you think? You want space and space means you don't want me. California is where you're going to go when you remove yourself from my life, so why not just do it now? Rip off the fucking Band-Aid and leave me in your rearview mirror."

"If you want me to leave, I will go."

Simon waves his arm at me dismissively as he rolls onto his side, curling up in the fetal position. "Do whatever the fuck you want, Stella. You were going to do that from the start anyways."

He falls silent and I don't push any harder. He's drunk so I should take what he's saying with a grain of salt. I should just crawl back into bed and let him sleep it off and reevaluate in the morning, but I can't. I can't fucking do it.

My chest aches and there's a hole in the shape of Simon there. He ripped my heart from my chest, clutching it in his hand while it was beating, before he tore it to shreds and discarded it on the floor.

I'm struggling with my feelings and how to separate my emotions in a rational way. It doesn't take me long to pack my things and change into a pair of sweatpants and pull a hoodie over my t-shirt. Grabbing my phone, I open up the Uber app and put in the address of the airport as my destination.

I have nowhere to go in California right now. I don't even know if I'll be able to get a flight tonight, but I know that I can't stay here any longer. There's no place for me here. I overstayed my welcome and pushed Simon to the point that he's doing exactly what he said he wouldn't do. He's letting me go, and I don't know if he even realizes it.

He's passed out, snoring lightly as I look over at him once more through my tears. I leave him behind, leaving the key I was using on the counter next to his before I let myself out of the apartment. When I reach the first floor, my Uber is already here and there's no turning back at this point.

I asked him for space and he's giving me thousands of miles of distance instead. The tears don't stop as I climb into the Uber and thankfully, my driver doesn't ask me what's wrong.

Simon said he wasn't Trey, and he was right. He's much worse than Trey ever was.

I never loved my ex-boyfriend.

CHAPTER TWENTY-EIGHT
SIMON

My head pounds as I slowly begin to wake up the next morning. I slowly peel my eyes open, feeling the burn from the sun that shines brightly through the apartment windows.

"Fuck," I mumble, pulling a pillow over my face to block out the light. It's too much and a wave of nausea rolls through my stomach. I drank a lot more than I planned last night and I'm really regretting it right now.

I don't fully remember getting back here and I sure as hell don't remember ending up on the couch. It's been my new bed so it's not surprising, but it's too quiet in the apartment. Something feels weird and off. Pulling the pillow away from my face, I squint my eyes against the sunlight and my head screams in protest as I sit up.

It feels like I was hit by an eighteen-wheeler and I can feel it in every fiber of my body. I don't know the last time I felt hungover like this but in this moment, I swear I will never drink again. Jesus Christ.

Turning around on the couch, I glance over at the bed, expecting to see Stella, but she isn't there. The covers are thrown back in a haste, like she quickly climbed out of bed in a rush. I instantly get a head-rush as I turn to look around the rest of the studio apartment. I can see every part of it from where I'm sitting.

And there isn't a single sign of Stella.

The bathroom door is open, so I know she isn't in there. Panic washes over me, mixing with a nauseous feeling in the pit of my stomach. *Where the hell is she?*

It's a Saturday morning. Unless she went for a walk, I have no idea where she would be. Grabbing my phone, I check to see if she texted me to let me know, but there's nothing from her. It takes every ounce of energy that I can muster to get off the couch and walk around the apartment.

As I walk toward the bedroom, that's when reality slaps me in the fucking face.

She's gone.

All of her things are gone. My feet move quickly, carrying me over to her dresser. I rip open drawer after drawer, the wood creaking and breaking as I do, and I find each and every one empty. Looking under the bed, I see that her suitcase is gone.

I jump up, ignoring the way the room spins and bile rises in my throat. I move around the apartment frantically, looking for any sign of hope that maybe —*maybe*—she didn't actually leave.

Everything is gone from the bathroom. And when I step into the kitchen, my entire world crumbles to my feet as I see her key sitting right next to mine on the counter. I can't stop the bile as it quickly rises and I rush over to the sink, reaching it just in time to spill the contents of my stomach down the drain.

I don't stop until I'm bent over, dry heaving. My stomach lurches until there's nothing left to come out. My entire chest is on fire and my throat burns from the damage I've just done to it. Combined with all the alcohol I drank last night and finding Stella gone, there was no way I could have stopped it from happening.

I'm out of breath as I stand upright and run the water, rinsing my mouth out before wiping it with a paper towel. Turning around, I press my back against the counter and let myself slide down the cabinets until I'm sitting on the floor. Folding my legs, my knees are by my face and I hang my head heavily between them.

"Where the hell did you go, angel?" I mumble out loud as I pull out my phone and scroll through it. I find the message thread between us and send her at least five in a row. Each one simply just says *delivered.*

Tapping on her name, I press the phone icon to try and call her. It goes directly to voicemail.

"Fuck!" I yell out, chucking my phone across the room. It hits the back of the couch and falls to the floor with a loud thud. I don't even care. The entire screen could be shattered and the damn thing could stop working.

It doesn't fucking matter, not if Stella is gone.

———

"What do you mean you don't know where she went?" Olivia questions me through the phone. Sterling was the first person I could think to call.

Stella is his sister and his fiancée is Stella's best friend. One of them has to know where she is.

"I woke up and she was gone."

Olivia is silent for a beat and Sterling still hasn't said anything. "Okay... do you remember anything that happened last night? Why would she just up and leave like that?"

I'm sitting on the couch and I rest my forehead against my palm with my elbow propped up on my knee. "I was upset about how things were between us and I went to the bar and got shit-faced. I honestly don't remember much of what happened after I got home. Just bits and pieces."

"Well, what happened? Maybe that can give us an idea of where she might be."

This is the second time I'm on the phone with Olivia today. I called her a little bit ago and she promptly tried to call Stella, but she ran into the same issue that I did. Her phone is still turned off. Sterling reached out to their mother but she hadn't heard from Stella either.

Sitting in silence, I close my eyes as I replay the night before through my mind. It's like quickly scrolling through a video tape that had been damaged. I don't remember a lot of what was said between the two of us. Hell, there's a lot of gaps, thanks to the alcohol, but there's one thing that sticks out in my mind.

And as soon as I remember the words, I instantly regret them and hate myself.

"Fuck…"

"What is it?" Olivia questions me with panic in her voice.

I swallow roughly and open my eyes, staring blankly at the wall across from me. "I told her that she should just go back to California."

Sterling finally speaks and tense tone slices through the silence. "Why the hell would you do that?"

He has every right to be pissed off at me right now. Hell, I'm equally mad at myself for what I said to her. And that's just the one thing that sticks out in my mind. I know I told her I was in love with her, but that doesn't even matter at this point. I'm sure me telling her to leave practically washed away me professing my love for her.

I've never felt more regret in my entire life before. "I don't fucking know," I admit with a defeated sigh. "I was drunk and I guess I let my emotions get the better of me. I have no clue why I would say something that goddamn stupid."

"Yeah, and you should know Stella well enough

by now to know she took that to heart." Olivia pauses for a brief second, whispering something to Sterling in the background. "She may act like she doesn't care about stuff sometimes, but her hearing that probably made her run."

"You're a fucking idiot," Sterling scoffs. "You better make it up to her, Simon. I'm not blind or stupid. I've known about the two of you since that one night when you went upstairs together. Stella and I might not always get along, but she's my sister. I have no problem fucking you up if you fuck her over."

Sterling is right, but I was too drunk last night to think about it. Although the thought had definitely crossed my mind this past week, it's not something I planned to ever say to Stella. It wasn't a thought that I would have actually entertained enough to wish it into existence.

Abruptly, I rise to my feet, putting Olivia and Sterling's call on speakerphone as I walk over to the bedroom area. Grabbing a backpack from under the bed, I begin to throw clothing into it. I take the bag in my hand and move around my apartment, grabbing the essentials I will need. I don't know how long I'll be gone, but a change or two of clothes should be enough.

"Are you still there?" Olivia's voice breaks through the silence.

"Yep, I'm just packing some shit."

She's silent for a fraction of a second. "What are you doing, Simon?"

Picking up my phone, I open a new tab in Safari and begin to search for flights. I find the first one that's leaving from the closest airport and select it. It leaves in approximately two hours so I need to hightail it to the airport.

"I'm going to California and getting my girl back."

"Don't fuck this up, Simon," Sterling warns me.

Fuck this hockey camp. Fuck the tournaments that are set to begin in literally two days' time. The only thing that matters right now is making things right with Stella, and hopefully winning her back.

"Don't worry," I assure him. "I won't."

I'm about to play the most important game of my life.

And I play to fucking win.

CHAPTER TWENTY-NINE
STELLA

My parents are going to be pissed about the credit card charges for this hotel room, but I was left with no other options. First on my list is to find a job. I don't know if I'll be able to find one that will pay well enough for me to cover the expense of my hotel room, but it's worth a shot.

I only have a few weeks left until I'll be able to move back into my dorm room. So, if I want to be on the West Coast rather than the East, this is the only way I am going to be able to make it work. It's not like I picked an expensive hotel, either. I found one that is a short Uber ride away from the airport and it is one that isn't dumpy, but it isn't a Four Seasons either.

It's around noontime when I finally turn my phone back on. I turned it off when I got here in the middle of the night and didn't bother turning it back on until now. The last thing I wanted to do was have to talk to anyone. I'm sure after Simon woke up this morning and realized I was gone, he put in a call to my brother.

As soon as my phone loads everything on it, I'm not surprised when the missed calls and unread text messages come rolling in. I ignore anything that has Simon's name on it, only paying attention to the ones from my parents and Sterling and Olivia.

I send a quick text to my mom to let her know that I'm alive and back in California and that I will explain everything to her soon. She doesn't respond right away so I move on to Olivia's. There's at least a dozen texts from her, the last one reading 911.

A sigh escapes me as I tap on her name and the phone begins to ring. She picks up after one ring.

"Stella!" she exclaims, her voice loud and filled with relief. "Thank God. I was beginning to really worry about you."

"I'm fine," I assure her. "I turned my phone off on the plane and when I got to my hotel, I passed out and didn't even think to turn it back on."

"Where are you? Simon called and told us you were gone."

A lump forms in my throat, but I swallow back my emotions and lock them tightly away in the box they belong in. "Yeah, I flew back to California in the middle of the night."

"He told me what he said, that he told you to go back to California." She pauses and falls silent for a short moment. "What really happened?"

"It was all my fault," I explain, feeling like a deflated balloon and filled with defeat. "I made things weird between us. Simon wanted more and I told him I needed space. I needed to figure out how the hell things would work between us."

"You didn't want to get involved if you knew you were going to get hurt in the end, I get it."

I nod, even though Olivia can't see me through the phone. "Exactly. So, he decided to give me space and then he came back last night completely shit-faced and said a lot of things I know he had probably been holding in."

Olivia's silent for a beat. "I know you might think that, but that's not Simon. He wouldn't say things like that and actually mean it. He gets emotional when he's drunk."

"Well, he still said them and seemed pretty serious about it."

"What else did he say to you?"

The nightmare plays over in my head again. "He told me that he's in love with me and I was breaking his heart. He interpreted me wanting space as me trying to buy myself some time to let him down easy."

"Ugh," Olivia groans. "These stupid guys. They always assume shit and it's like their pride gets the better of them. Instead of talking it through with us, they just interpret and run with it."

"That's exactly what Simon did. He really left me no choice."

"Did he really, though?" Olivia questions me, the challenge clear in her voice. "You didn't have to run. You could have waited until morning to hear him out."

I swallow roughly. "It was better if I left then, Liv."

"It was your fear that made you run."

I don't respond. Instead we settle into a silence, both of us knowing that she's right. I did let my fear take control and that was ultimately what made me leave for the airport in the middle of the night.

"What hotel are you staying at?" Olivia questions me, her voice sounding defeated.

"The Hilton on Main," I tell her before reciting the address. "Why? My mom knows I'm here and I have to talk to her about staying here until I can go back to my dorm."

"What room?"

Her questions throw me off and my eyebrows draw together. "713. Why, Olivia?"

Olivia doesn't say anything for a bit. "Simon is on a plane to California right now. I told him that I would find out where you are."

My breath catches in my throat. "What? Why the hell is he coming here? What about his camp? Their tournament is supposed to start on Monday."

"Yeah, I know," she says with a sigh. "He left it all to come find you."

"What the hell? Why would he throw that all away? I can't let him do that."

"Because he loves you, you idiot," she tells me with annoyance in her tone. She lets out a contradictory light laugh. "Good luck trying to stop him. He's on his way to you now, Stella. Either end things with him or bury your fear and take the leap with him."

Tears begin to blur my vision without my permission. "I'm afraid, Olivia. How did you know that Sterling was worth the risk? You're giving up everything for him."

"It might seem that way, but I'm really not. I just know what Sterling's dreams are and will always support them," she tells me and I can hear the smile in her voice. "I knew he was worth the risk when he showed me that I was more important to him than hockey."

"Just like Simon is doing right now…"

Olivia laughs softly. "Exactly."

"What do I do now?" I question her, my voice quiet as panic starts to build inside. Simon is on his way here and I'm not prepared at all.

She laughs again. "You buckle up and hold on for one hell of a ride. His plane should be landing around four. Leave your phone on this time because he'll be calling you when he's on his way."

"Oh my god. I'm going to have an anxiety attack, Olivia." I rise to my feet and begin to pace. "I left, like, twelve hours ago. Who the hell flies across the country to win someone back?"

"Just breathe, Stella. It's only Simon," she reminds me with that damn smile in her voice again. "He's just coming to collect you and your heart. And I think it's fairly safe to say that both belong to him."

My heart swells in my chest at the thought of

Simon. He put his entire hockey career in jeopardy to come find me. Part of me regrets leaving, had I known he would pull some stunt like this…

I smile at the phone.

"They do, because I'm in love with him, Liv."

CHAPTER THIRTY
SIMON

As I walk through the gate and into the airport, my phone vibrates from my pocket. I pull it out and see a message from Olivia. She has the name of the hotel and the address where Stella is, along with her room number.

Either her or Sterling must have been able to get through to Stella. I don't know what Olivia had to do to get that information, but I will forever be indebted to her. There's a part of me that is surprised she actually got it.

Stella could have just stayed with me in Canada instead of running the entire way back to California. This is the situation we're in now and I need her to give me a chance to explain myself. I need to find a way to get her to forgive me for the shit I said.

And I'm going to make sure she knows the truth behind some of my words.

Even though I was drunk, I meant what I said about being in love with her. I tried as hard as I could to prevent it from happening and I failed miserably. This might be my last chance to shoot my shot with her and I'm not about to fuck it up.

I send Olivia a message back, thanking her and telling her that I'll let her know how it goes. Opening up my Uber app, I put in the address that Olivia gave me and select the car. The driver who picks it up is only five minutes away so I lengthen my strides before I'm standing outside of the airport, waiting for my ride in the parking lot.

Opening up my messages, I tap on Stella's name and begin to type her a message.

SIMON

I'm coming for you, angel.

The Uber pulls up and I lock my screen before hopping into the back seat. It's only an eight-minute car ride to where the hotel is. I realistically could have walked, but I have no idea where the hell I am.

Taking an Uber just made a lot more sense in the moment.

But right now, I just want to get to Stella as fast as I can.

I stare at the black screen on my phone, waiting for it to light up from a message coming through, but it doesn't. I don't even know if she read my message. None of that matters, though. I'm already on my way to her and I'm not so sure she's going to be happy to see me after the way I acted last night.

Before I know it, we're pulling up to the hotel and I'm throwing the driver a cash tip before making my way through the front doors. My phone vibrates, catching me off guard as I wait for the elevator to make its way down to the lobby.

STELLA

I've been waiting for you.

SIMON

You never should have left, Stella.

STELLA

Where are you? We'll talk when you get here.

The elevator dings as it reaches the lobby and the doors slide open. I step inside and press the button for her floor. As the doors slide shut, I type out my last message to Stella.

SIMON

On my way up the elevator now.

When I reach Stella's floor, my feet carry me down the hall until I'm standing outside of her door. Lifting my hand, I lightly knock on it, and she must be waiting on the other side for me because I hear the lock turning and Stella pulls the door open.

She's standing there, no makeup on, her hair in a messy bun... and she's wearing one of my t-shirts. My heart clenches as I take in the sight of her and I swear it crawls into my fucking throat, restricting my airflow. I didn't even notice that it was missing when I was packing in a frenzy earlier today.

She took it for a reason and I'm a mess of emotions, dying to know what the reasoning behind it truly was.

"Did you want to come in?" Stella asks me, her voice quiet as she shifts her weight nervously on her feet.

"Absolutely."

Stella steps out of the way, pulling the door open farther as she makes room for me to walk in. As I step past her, I catch the smell of her perfume and it invades my senses, tapping deep into my memory. The way she smells is something I'll never be able to eradicate from my mind.

I just want to feel her body close to mine. I just want things to go back to how they were before.

After walking through the doorway, I stop short in the small hallway, waiting as she shuts the door and locks it behind me. She gives me a small smile, walking past me. I stalk after her, following her lead as we walk into the hotel room. It's not anything extravagant and I'm a little surprised she's in a hotel instead of staying with someone here.

Stella walks over to her bed, sitting down on the edge of it. Across from where she's sitting is a small table with two chairs. I walk over, taking my backpack off and set it down on the floor as I take a seat on one of the chairs. As much as I would love to sit closer to her, I feel like this is where I belong.

I don't want to overstep any boundaries or make her feel like I'm coming on too strong.

She folds her hands in her lap, her eyes meeting mine. "I'm sorry that I left. I should have stayed and waited to talk to you this morning. It was irrational and impulsive."

"You're not the one who should be apologizing, Stella," I tell her, my voice soft as I desperately search her eyes. "I'm the one who fucked up. I said some fucked-up things that I didn't mean while I was drunk."

She swallows hard and nods. "I know. That's why I should have waited to talk to you about it after you sobered up."

"There's something I need to tell you."

Stella stares at me, her eyes widening slightly. She looks like she doesn't know what to expect and that makes my stomach do a somersault. "Okay," she says quietly, a hesitancy in her voice.

Leaning forward, I rest my forearms on my knees as I stare up at Stella. "There were some things I said that I didn't mean, but there were also some that held truth behind them." I let out a deep breath, my eyes desperately searching hers. "I'm in love with you, Stella. I've been in love with you for a long fucking time now, I was just trying so hard to ignore it. I can't ignore it any longer and I can't keep lying to myself and you. I'm hopelessly in love with you, and I can't imagine my life without you."

There's a moment of silence and it feels like time is suspended as I watch the realization dawn over her. There's a flash of relief in her eyes, one of hope and another of absolute fright.

"You're not supposed to fall in love with me,

Simon," she reminds me, her voice barely above a whisper. "This was just supposed to be a summer thing while I was on my journey to figure out who I am and what I want in life."

"Fuck that," I tell her, abruptly rising to my feet as I close the distance between us. "I've given you space and I've given you time. I know what I want, Stella, and that's you. I want to do life with you. I don't give a shit what sacrifices I have to make in order for that to happen. Let yourself fall. Experience life. Experience love. Experience it all with me."

Her throat bobs as she swallows, then she stands up, her frame much smaller than mine. She tilts her head backward to look up at me. "I'm in love with you too, Simon," she admits, tilting her head to the side. "You are what I want. I was afraid because the thought of the future hurts my stomach. There's no guarantee and I don't know what it looks like between us, but I don't care anymore. We can figure that all out. And if things don't work out in the end, at least I had the chance to be loved by you."

"We will figure it out and we will make it work, angel," I tell her as I step into her space and cup the sides of her face. "Whatever has to happen, I will make it happen. As long as you're in my life, the rest of it doesn't matter."

"What about hockey? What about when you make it pro?"

I raise an eyebrow. "What about it? I thought that was my life, but I was wrong. I didn't realize what was the most important thing to me until you became such a focal point of my life."

"And what's that?" she questions me, her voice soft.

The corners of my lips lift upward. "You." My face dips down to hers, my lips brushing against hers. "None of my accomplishments with hockey matter if I don't have you to celebrate them with."

"You shouldn't even be here right now," she reminds me, pulling back enough to look up at me. "You're supposed to be back at camp. The tournament starts on Monday..."

"None of that matters without you," I tell her with nothing but love and honesty in my voice. "I had to come find you. I needed to know we still had a chance."

"If I tell you that we do, will you stop being stupid and go back to Canada so you can play what you've worked all summer for?"

I stare down at her as she stares directly into my soul. "If you come back with me."

"To Canada?"

I nod. "Come finish the summer there with me and then come home, back to Vermont. Come be where you belong—with me."

Stella smiles up at me. "Okay."

My eyebrows tug together. "Wait, seriously?"

"Yes, seriously," Stella giggles. "I'll figure out transferring to Wyncote University on Monday. I'll come back with you, Simon. If this summer and flying back to California has taught me anything, it's that you are my home and I don't want to be apart from you."

Tugging on her, I pull her flush against my body. "I love you, Stella Barrett. Tell me that you'll be mine."

She lifts up onto her tiptoes, her lips brushing against mine. "I've always been yours, Simon. And I always will be."

EPILOGUE
SIMON

"You're acting weird, Simon," Stella tells me as she stares at me from across the kitchen. "Why won't you tell me where we're going?"

I stare at her, my frustration growing. Stella isn't exactly the best when it comes to surprises or keeping any kind of secret. I found this out this Christmas when I caught her snooping through her gifts. And then when she insisted she give me her gift, like, three days after she got it for me.

Which was two weeks before Christmas.

So, yeah... trying to surprise Stella without her demanding to know where we are going or what is going on is quite a challenge. I'm already nervous as hell about what I have planned for tonight and her challenging it all isn't easing any of my anxiety.

"I'm not acting weird, angel," I assure her, struggling to keep my voice on an even keel. "Just please go get dressed? I made dinner reservations and we have to leave in five minutes if we want to get there on time."

Stella narrows her eyes but she doesn't say anything more before she disappears from the room. I can't stop the stupid grin from pulling on my lips, knowing I just won that little tiff. I'm sure she's going to make the car ride tense with her relentless questions, but I'm prepared. I think...

She's surprisingly ready to go in record time and greets me by the front door with a smile on her face instead of the scowl she was sporting earlier. Stella's mood did a complete one-eighty and as we head out to my car, she's talking about how her brother and his new wife are doing in Maine.

After we spent the summer in Canada, Stella moved back to Vermont and transferred to Wyncote University. She's still in her sophomore year, but none of that matters to either of us. I would be graduating at the end of this school year and I already know that I won't be going anywhere without Stella.

Talk of the NHL is still floating around and quite a few scouts have me on their list, but I haven't heard of anything in regards to what team I am most likely going to get drafted to. Stella already expressed her wanting to support me and that she would go wherever I would end up.

Even though there was a point where hockey was the most important thing to me, some things have shifted in my life. I wouldn't be making any decisions without talking to Stella first. Her wants and needs are equally important to me.

"Olivia said that we need to come visit them soon," Stella tells me from where she's sitting in my passenger seat. I glance over at her, my lips pulling upward. She's exactly where she belongs.

"Whatever you want to do, angel. If you want to go visit them, you just tell me when and I'll get it all planned."

She looks over at me with a matching smile. "I love you, Simon."

"And I love you that much more, Stella."

She moved into the house with Lincoln and me when she moved back to Vermont. Instead of taking her brother's old room, she moved into mine, and there was no going back after that. Stella is a permanent fixture in my life and I have no intention of her ever leaving it.

When we pull up in front of the restaurant, we are able to find a parking spot right out front. It's one of Stella's favorites and it's a damn hard one to get into. It's a French restaurant that only has twenty tables inside. It's more of an experience than anything. I had to make reservations two months ago just for tonight.

And it's been killing me keeping this entire night a damn secret until now.

I walk over and open the door for Stella, holding my hand out to her. She smiles up at me as she slides her palm into mine and I help her out of the car before shutting the door behind her. Pushing the button on my key fob, the car beeps, and I slide it into my pocket as we head toward the restaurant.

As we step inside, different smells touch my senses. The restaurant is dimly lit with a very intimate atmosphere. Light classical music plays softly through the speaker system and Stella turns to face me as we stand just inside.

"You remembered this place."

I smile down at her, brushing a piece of her hair from her face as I tuck it behind her ear. "I could never forget."

I've never been here before and Stella had talked about it so many times. She was only ever here once before and it's a place that easily slid into the number one spot of her favorites. With how hard it was to get a reservation, I am not surprised that she wasn't able to come again. And we tried to make a reservation before this one and weren't able to.

That's when the idea came to me.

Stella turns around, her eyebrows pulling together as she glances around the empty restaurant. "There's no one here," she says softly as she turns back to me. "What's going on?"

"I paid for us to have a private dining experience for an hour."

Stella's eyes widen. "You did what? That had to have cost a fortune."

A chuckle escapes me and I shake my head as I take a step toward my girl. "Don't worry about any of that. You deserve so much more than this."

She stares at me, her mouth falling open as I take her hand and lower myself onto one knee in front of her. Releasing her hand, I slide mine into my front pocket and pull out the small black velvet box that has been burning a hole in it since I bought it three months ago.

"Oh my god, Simon," she gasps, lifting her hands

to cover her mouth as I flip open the lid and meet her gaze.

"I was going to wait until after dinner to do this, but I've been waiting long enough. I don't think I could wait any fucking longer."

Tears well in her eyes as they desperately search mine. I'm overwhelmed with emotion, my body buzzing as my tongue darts out to wet my lips. Stella doesn't say anything as she smiles down at me, her mascara staining her cheeks.

"I can't imagine life without you, Stella Barrett. I don't know what it looks like without you in it anymore. I want the rest of your days, the rest of your kisses. I want every goddamn moment with you and I want it as you being Stella Murray."

"Simon," her voice cracks and she lets out a soft laugh, shaking her head at me. "You are unlike anyone else I've ever met in my life. Always full of surprises."

"Let me spoil you, angel. Let me love you. Let me make you my fucking wife."

She smiles down at me through her tears. "Of course. Yes. I'll marry you, Simon."

Stella drops down to her knees in front of me, wrapping her arms around my neck. It's a sight to see and isn't exactly how it usually happens. She throws me off-balance a little and I fall over onto my side, taking her with me. Stella yelps before a string of laughter falls from her perfect lips.

"You couldn't wait until I stood back up?" I ask her as we lay in a mess of tangled limbs on the floor of the restaurant.

Stella giggles and smiles at me. "I don't know. I just reacted."

Grabbing her hand, I slide the ring onto her finger before lifting it to my lips. "My angel."

"I love you," she murmurs, her voice thick with emotion.

Dropping her hand, I slide mine around the back of her neck, pulling her face to mine. "I will always love you more," I tell her before pressing my lips to hers.

SIMON AND STELLA BONUS SCENE

As I step out of the shower, I notice that there's silence throughout our suite. Wrapping a towel around my waist, I don't bother drying off before walking through the bathroom to look for my wife. Tonight was the last night of our honeymoon and the first one that Stella didn't end up in the shower with me.

I know they say that the honeymoon stage fizzles out eventually, but I don't see how that could ever possibly happen between the two of us. Not when I can't seem to get enough of her.

The entire suite is empty and my heart begins to pound erratically in my chest as I go over every bad scenario that could have possibly unfolded. The Cayman Islands are supposed to be safe but that doesn't help the anxious thoughts in my mind as I begin to frantically search for my wife.

Standing in the middle of the bedroom, I spin around once more, my breathing shallow and erratic. The curtains by the door that leads to our balcony shift in the wind and that's when I notice the doors are cracked open.

As I step out onto the balcony, I see Stella and a wave of relief washes over me. She's leaning against the railing, staring out at the soft ripples in the ocean as it laps against the shore. The moon hangs in the sky above, casting its light across the water.

Walking up behind her, I slide my hands along her arms before gripping her hands on the balcony railing. My lips brush the outer shell of her ear. "There you are, angel."

"It's our last night here," she says with sadness in her voice. "I wish I could stay here in paradise with you forever."

Releasing her hands, I slide mine back up her bare arms, feeling her soft skin under my fingertips. She's wearing nothing but a sheer piece of lingerie and I slowly untie the knot in the front before pushing the material away from her shoulders.

"You want to stay?" I murmur, trailing my lips

along the side of her neck. "Say the word and I'll have it arranged."

My cock is already hard, pressing through my towel. Stella bends at the waist, pushing her bare ass against me.

"I've just liked having you to myself," she breathes as I drag my tongue along her flesh. Pulling away, I stand up straight and spit into my hand for lube. I undo my towel and wrap my fingers around my cock, pumping it a few times to get my salvia coating it.

Pushing the tip against her center, I groan as I slowly push inside her. "You're a greedy girl. You don't want to share me with anyone else, do you?"

Stella moans as I fill her completely. "No," she breathes, shaking her head. "I don't want to share you with anyone, ever."

Wrapping one hand in her hair, I jerk her head back as I grip her hip with my other hand. "You know what I mean, angel." I soften my touch but pound into her again. "I'm yours. Forever and always. If you don't want to share me with anyone, I'd gladly lock the two of us away for an eternity."

"What about everything and everyone else?" she questions me breathlessly as I continue to fuck her on the balcony under the light of the moon.

"Fuck everyone else," I growl, slamming into her. "You're the only thing that matters. You're the most important part of my life." Releasing her hair, I let my hands wander across her body. "No more talking, angel. I want you to take my cock like the good girl you are."

She doesn't protest or speak another word. I watch her grip tighten on the railing of the balcony as I fuck her with no inhibitions. She's mine, for better or worse, in sickness and in health.

Stella Murray is mine for the rest of our lives.

NEXT IN THE SERIES

Off-Ice Collision is the eighth book from the Wyncote Wolves, featuring Vaughn and London. Continue reading below for a look inside Off-Ice Collision.

CHAPTER ONE
VAUGHN

The coldness radiates off the ice and it seeps through my socks as my skates effortlessly glide across the smooth surface. It's the first period and we're out on fresh ice with the start of the game. Usually August Whitley would be the starting center, but our coach has started alternating between the two of us.

Since I'm a freshman at Wyncote University, I don't get as much ice time as the seniors on our team do, but our coach knows that I need to be out there too. I've been looked at by scouts since I was in high school and if everything goes accordingly, I'll be playing on a professional level next season.

College won't even matter then, not that it did from the start. I only came here for the hockey program Wyncote has and the fact that it's one of the biggest hockey colleges. I declared my major as some bullshit business degree because in the end, it didn't really matter.

I was going to be playing professional hockey, so my college degree meant nothing.

It's time for the puck drop and I slide across the ice, stopping as I reach the center ring. The opposing center player is already crouched down and in the correct stance for the face-off. The rest of their team are already in their zones. I glance around, noting Sterling Barrett and Hayden King as they fall into place.

My eyes meet the other center's, Number 18, as I crouch down in front of him. Both of our sticks are in our hands and anticipation builds in the air as we wait for the ref to drop the puck. Time is suspended momentarily before I watch the black frozen piece of rubber begin to fall down between the two of us.

We battle over the puck, both of our sticks slapping at one another's as we're lost in a power struggle. One of us is going to win the face-off and I'm not going to be the one who skates away without one of my teammates having the puck. Using the toe of my skate, I lift up his stick, just quick enough for me to get the puck away from him before passing it back to Hayden.

I move out of the way, watching as Hayden takes the puck and begins to circle around. He starts to move in the direction of the opposing team's net. Sterling and I both begin to skate ahead of him, each of us taking opposite sides of the rink. Hayden passes the puck to Sterling and he doesn't miss a beat as he begins to stickhandle it, skating across the slick surface.

Hayden falls back, hanging back in the defensive zone as Sterling and I both continue to skate closer to the net. Sterling and I make eye contact and he sends the puck to me as another player approaches him. I'm already ahead of him and closer to the net. The muscles in my legs work harder as I skate faster, picking up speed with every stride I take.

The net is practically wide open with just the goaltender occupying the space in front of it. He's already dropped into a stance as he sees me charging at him. He's anticipating my next move and I know I need to fake him out.

Suddenly, one of the defensive players on their team enters my field of vision. I thought he was already preoccupied by someone else, but now he's directly in my way. Stick-handling the puck, I move it around as I attempt to confuse him on which way I'm going to skate around him. His bright yellow jersey sticks out and the number 8 is on the front.

I make a move like I'm going to the right and I watch as he begins to shift his weight before I switch to the left.

Number 8 matches my movements and he's quicker than I expected. Instead of attempting to take the puck from me, he slides his skate out to try and trip me. As he makes the move, he braces himself, and I don't even see it coming as my knee collides directly into his.

It's almost as if the entire thing happens in slow motion but I had no time to anticipate any of it. A searing pain erupts in my knee, tearing through my leg like wildfire. All movement ceases with that leg and it's essentially useless. I can't hold myself up and I crumble onto the ice, unable to bear any weight on my leg.

I fall onto my side with my injured left leg propped on top of my right leg. The bottom half of my leg feels like it is completely detached from the top, yet I can feel every goddamn nerve ending on fire from the pain. Tears well in my eyes and I blink rapidly, attempting to hold them back as my jaw clenches.

My surroundings begin to fade and the blackness grows around the perimeter of my vision. Planting my gloved hands on the ice, I attempt to lift myself back onto my feet, but as soon as my left skate touches the slick surface, pain slices through me. It radiates throughout my entire leg and I'm left breathless as I collapse back onto the ice.

"Shit," Hayden growls as he and Sterling are both

crouched down and in my face. "We gotta get you back to see the doc, bro."

Words fail me. I have nothing to say. Judging by the pain and the way that my leg feels, this is all over. Within the blink of a fucking eye, my future is ruined.

"Just leave me here," I mumble, attempting to push the two of them away. I'd rather die than never be able to play again.

"Come on, man," Sterling says as the two of them begin to slide their arms under me to lift me up. "We're not leaving you here. Can you bear any weight?"

Swallowing roughly, I shake my head. I don't know which hurts worse, the physical pain from my injury or the pain that licks at my heart right now. Hayden's jaw clenches and there's a solemnness to both his and Sterling's expressions. They hoist me up and I wrap my arms around the backs of their necks as they both take their positions on opposite sides of me.

They both slip their arms underneath my knees as they attempt to carry me off the ice. As Sterling puts pressure on the underside of my knee, the pain tears through my body and the intensity is too much. I yell out but my voice is quickly drowned out as everything around me goes black.

———

I wake up in a haste, drenched in my own sweat. My heart pounds erratically in my chest, rattling against my rib cage. It feels like the wind has been knocked out of me and I struggle to take in a deep breath. Sitting upright, I glance around the room, noticing that I'm in my bed at my parents' house.

My left knee throbs and I throw off the blanket as I glance down, hoping that it was all just a nightmare. The moonlight that shines through the window casts itself across my leg, revealing the angry, ugly scars on my leg. This—this is the real fucking nightmare.

It's been two years since my injury.

Two years since I last played ice hockey.

Two years since my life was forever changed.

And no matter how hard I try, it replays in my mind every goddamn night. It's almost as if the universe hasn't gotten enough pleasure from taking the one thing that mattered the most away from me. No. Instead, I have to be punished every time I close my eyes to fall asleep.

It's always the same dream. Step for step, the memory that is forever etched into my mind of the one day that ended my hockey career. I was literally just getting started; I hadn't even transitioned into the professional level yet and it was all ripped away from me before I had the chance to fully taste it.

Collapsing onto my back, I attempt to steady my heart and regulate my breathing. I'm afraid to close my eyes again and instead, I lie there, staring up at the ceiling until the sky is changing colors. First comes the deep blue, which then shifts into a pinkish orange tone as the sun is beginning to fully crest the horizon.

I don't bother moving when I hear everyone beginning to move around the massive house. My parents were gracious enough to let me come back to live with them after the incident. My knee was completely blown out and my ACL was shredded beyond repair. They had to take part of my hamstring and make a graft since they weren't able to salvage any of the original ligament.

That was an injury I could have potentially recovered from. It's not uncommon in sports, and I know people who have torn their ACLs before and continued to play. It was the severity of mine that was the real kicker. The muscles in my left thigh were fucked up from the force of the blow to my leg and there were splinter fractures in my femur. There was also damage done to the joint.

My leg was fucking ruined. It was a long road to

recovery with the different surgeries I had to undergo. Not to mention the months of physical therapy afterward. I'm still not one hundred percent, and I never will be. There's a lingering pain that decides to visit me on occasion. I walk with a slight limp now.

And you want to know what the motherfucker who did this to me got?

A goddamn two-minute penalty and a sprained knee.

ALSO BY CALI MELLE

ABOUT THE AUTHOR

Cali Melle is a contemporary romance author who loves writing stories that will pull at your heart-strings. You can always expect her stories to come fully equipped with heartthrobs and a happy ending, along with some steamy scenes and some sports action. In her free time, Cali can usually be found with her nose in a book or freezing at the ice rink while she watches her kids play hockey and figure skate.